DARKEST CORNERS OF TEXAS

An Al Quinn Novel

RUSS HALL

Darkest Corners of Texas

An Al Quinn™ Mystery

Red Adept Publishing, LLC

104 Bugenfield Court

Garner, NC 27529

https://RedAdeptPublishing.com/

---

1.   http://StreetlightGraphics.com

The one true thing in life, if you are living on the very most dangerous edge of it, is that the next few seconds could go brilliantly bright... or as dark as it ever gets.

Chapter One

His shirt off, Al Quinn had crammed himself down into the dark, dank back end of his bass boat, prying and wrenching with his fingers at a bilge pump that had become clogged and burned out. *Fried.*

"Do you want me to switch on the radio and get some sweatin'-with-the-oldies music playing?" Fergie stood over him, aiming a flashlight into the aft hold so that he could see what he was doing.

The sun burned hot and yellow in a stark blue sky over her shoulder.

"Don't forget you're the same age as me," he said.

Al tugged out the last of the old defunct pump, having suffered only a scuffed knuckle or two. He set the dead pump on the aft deck and started cleaning the area below. The new pump sat in its box nearby, waiting to be installed.

"Well, I'm sweating up here just watching you work away in the hot guts of that boat," she said.

Al glanced up. Fergie was wearing a fairly skimpy bright-green bikini, and a brisk gust was fanning out her long red hair. Her skin had a light, shiny patina of brightness, but he would hardly call that sweating hard. She sure didn't look his age. Sheriff Clayton liked to kid Al that he was the fittest retired person he'd ever seen, but Fergie's lean, athletic body made her look a helluva lot younger than him.

They'd once shared what they now referred to as the worst date in the history of high school proms—a category with numerous entries. The experience had vigorously bounced them apart for many years, most of which she ended up working as a detective for the city police while he did his detecting with the county. He hadn't expected them to ever wind up together. *Look at us now.*

"Uh oh," she said, reaching for her beach robe, which hung from the steering wheel. "Company's coming." After tugging her robe on, she bent low into the boat. When she stood again, her robe pulled lower on the right side from the weight of the Glock she'd slipped into her pocket.

He nodded. *You never know.* He heard the roar of a boat heading their way—sounded like the big motor of a cigarette boat, something like that.

Her tone and getting the gun had told him enough. He didn't need to ask if he should pull himself away from his task. Al climbed up out of his hole.

She handed him a rag then held out his shirt once he'd wiped the grease and dirt off his hands. He didn't care much if he got that shirt dirty. It was one of several he kept at the back of his closet, tattered and worn, for doing just such chores around the house or to wear when he took his vehicle to the mechanic so that he wouldn't look too prosperous and get billed for a bunch of stuff he didn't need.

He looked across the lake and saw the white spray of a rooster tail the boat was putting up as it crossed the lake, coming right toward them. The wind was mounting little whitecaps on the waves across the otherwise blue-green water. The breeze brought the smell of the lake to him, slightly fishy... in a good way, which made him glad to be alive. He wanted to get the boat fixed so he could lower it into the water and they could be off fishing. But fixing the broken bilge was taking longer than expected.

He liked living by a lake and especially being out on it, even when he wasn't catching fish, feeling the vigorous tug on the line as a bass struck his lure. He would feel a surge of joy. Just being on the water, feeling the breeze, hearing the steady waves, and seeing the shoreline was enough for him some days. If he saw an osprey or a line of turtles back to Al, some of the old anger issues were rippling across Dom's face. A flush of red climbed up from his chin to sweep across that bald dome, and his fingers curled into fists. Al was remembering a time when Dom had pulled a guy's arm off and beaten him with it. *Happy times.*

He turned to Fergie slowly, with all the menace he was capable of. Her robe had opened partially, and his eyes swept up and down the small strip of her trim body that was exposed. Then Dom noticed the gun Fergie held in one steady hand, pointing toward his chest.

"So it's gonna be like that, eh?" Dom's face showed a flash of a snarl.

"Exactly like that," Al said.

The fingers of Dom's fists uncurled. He shook his head and turned toward Al. "The boy still has a lot to learn."

"Yep. Being big isn't everything. Being quick counts for something."

"Big makes a bigger splash, though," Dom said, his mouth trying to twist into a smile as he went to the edge of the dock and held out a hand to help his nephew back up onto it.

Al had a few things he could have said about that, but he heard shouting from up at his house. He glanced up the hill toward it. His brother, Maury, came running down the walk beside the house and appeared beside the lower back porch, waving his arms in the air.

"What fresh new hell is this?" Fergie muttered.

"It's Tanner!" Maury yelled. "Someone just took off with him."

Al spun to Dom. "This isn't any of your doing, is it?"

Big as he was, Dom shook his head vigorously. "Me? No way."

"Just be gone when I get back." Al took off at a run toward the house.

Al glanced back. Fergie stayed on the deck with her gun still held out and pointed until the two thugs got back into the cigarette boat and fired up its big engine. They headed back across the lake as fast as the boat could take them.

Once they were gone, he ran around the side of his house to his truck and climbed inside.

He didn't have time to go inside to tell Bonnie and Little Al where he was going and make sure they stayed safe. Fergie could tend to that.

"Wait. Wait!" Maury yelled. He swung the passenger side door open and hopped inside.

Al took off in a spray of gravel before Maury could even slam the door.

He had it shut by the time Al had the truck out to the road. "Left," he said.

"What happened, Maury?"

"I was walking Tanner. A black van pulled up, and two guys hopped out. They grabbed Tanner's leash, hauled him away from me, and towed him toward the back of the van."

"Did Tanner try to bite them?"

"Of course he did."

"Well, good for him."

"But they lifted him by his leash, choking him, and threw him in the back. Then they took off."

"How long ago did this happen?"

"Just before I came yelling for you."

Al pressed down hard on the gas pedal. The truck slid a bit on the turns, but Al kept the throttle open all the way on the few straight stretches. Maury glanced his way but said nothing. Al's clenched jaws were telling him all he needed to know.

The truck gripped the road hard in a turn and started up a hill. As it surged over the top, Al caught a glimpse of the black van just cresting the curving hill ahead. He pressed harder on the gas.

"Al?"

"It's going to have to wait, Maury."

Chapter Two

Al and Maury moved back to his truck, out of the way of the deputies, who were still going over the place with an intensity that seemed a bit frenzied for such small-time criminals. They were poking about inside the buildings and looking all around the property. A department animal control truck pulled up, and that deputy led out the eleven dogs found behind the house in a chain-link enclosure. If Al hadn't acted like a hysterical parent, Tanner would have probably ended up with them to round out their number to an even dozen.

Al sat in the driver's seat of his truck with the door open. Tanner curled up on his lap, and Al felt him over. He couldn't feel any broken bones and got only a mild yip from Tanner when he brushed against one of the abrasions that would need cleaning and perhaps patching up. What he wanted to do above everything else was to make a quick trip to the vet to have her look Tanner over. But Victor Kahlon had said to wait. Sheriff Clayton himself was headed out to that desolate excuse for a ranch home and wanted to have words with Al.

That didn't bode well for Al—a rare instance of Clayton stirring from his office to come out himself, along with wanting to talk to him. From the looks Victor and the other deputies were giving him, he knew he'd stepped right into a real cow pie of an investigation. Al remembered how he'd felt when the same thing happened to him as an active detective—someone blowing his cover while he was on a stakeout, that sort of thing.

Victor spent some time with the two Stickley brothers, Brett and Bo, before they were hauled away to jail in one of the cruisers.

Thirty minutes after Al had come busting down the lane, he saw the dirt cloud kicked up by another cruiser as Clayton himself arrived, alone behind the wheel. He'd made really good time. Clayton put on his hat as he climbed out of the car, the dust still settling around it. He shook his head, and the corner of his mouth was twisted upward as he strode as big as John Wayne toward Al.

"Al Quinn. Al Quinn. Why in the blue-eyed devil do you pop up every time we're trying to pick and pull at some fragile loose end to something bigger?"

"They stole my dog," Al said.

"Well, they're damned lucky Victor was on hand, or we would've been sorting out the pieces cast far and wide of those unlikely two Stickley brothers right now."

"I might have rattled them like maracas, but I doubt I would have done more harm than that."

Clayton glanced toward Maury and Tanner. "Past circumstances seem to indicate otherwise. You have put the final punctuation on your share of hard cases."

"Only when they threatened my family, friends, or me," Al said. "And family includes Tanner."

"If anyone had told me a halfway hermit like you would have a family these days, they could have knocked me over with a loud burp. Yet it's turning out to be a regular hippie hive out at your place."

"Hey," Maury objected.

"What's going on here?" Al waved a hand toward the house, where the deputies and Victor were still busy inside. "Dog stealing seems pretty minor league."

Clayton glanced at the deputies, who still seemed to be looking for something. Victor pulled away from them and headed toward Al's truck.

"We've got something going on that may seem fuzzy around the edges at first," Clayton said, turning back to Al. "Victor is prone to take off on these little *ad hoc* whims of an investigation, kind of the way you used to do. It was probably a mistake for me to ask you to help train him. See what I get?"

Victor came to stand beside Clayton. He looked in at Al and the dog in his lap. "My ears were tingling. Were you all talking about me?"

"Why don't you explain to Al how you happen to be staked out at the spread of a third-rate pair of dognappers like the Stickleys, using up resources and getting few results."

"I might have gotten more results if not interrupted." Victor glanced at Al.

"I doubt it," Clayton said. "Go ahead. It's your rodeo out here."

Victor leaned in closer. He looked over at Maury and took in Tanner. Then his eyes lifted to fix on Al's. "I'm onto something sort of like the air-guitar cases you used to follow, hazy at first but slowly congealing into a slightly clearer picture. I have mostly loose threads at this point, but I'm gathering up a lot of threads."

Al glanced toward Clayton.

"Give him as much as you can," Clayton said. "His twisted head probably works more like yours than mine does."

"You're right in thinking this is pretty small-time," Victor said. "They had almost a dozen blue heelers in a pen out back. Animal control will see if any have microchips and match the rest to missing-dog reports."

"What did they plan to do with them?"

"Sell them. A buyer was already set up, waiting in the wings."

"Nickels and dimes," Al said. "Why?"

"It's the 'how' that's most interesting here. These guys are nobodies with short sheets of past crimes. But someone got in touch with them and told them what to do and how it would turn into money for them. They were just getting started."

"Zoom to the big picture." Clayton glanced at his watch.

"I started keeping track of this sort of thing, the MO," Victor said. "Small-timers getting steered and controlled to make money off stuff that doesn't go head-to-head with the big players or the cartels and their puppets. These guys and their small-time crimes fly under the radar of most law enforcement and the competition. And there are a lot of them I've identified with this pattern. They're instructed where to turn in the cut for the steering, and it's always a different place and usually a different method. Like you said, it's small change, but it adds up for someone. In the end, we're talking about serious money here, and a wave of these petty crimes."

"Are some of the bigger players starting to feel a pinch enough to go after these Stickley types?"

"You bet, and it's getting them nowhere."

"That might explain a visit I had this morning." Al turned to Clayton. "Do you know who Dom Strobinsky is working for these days?"

Clayton came very close to grinning. "He was picked up at the prison gate by a limo belonging to Kemper Giles."

"Is Kemper still squeaky clean?"

Clayton nodded. "But getting richer every day. The rub is he pays taxes for way more than someone with a landscaping firm could ever earn. We can keep an eye on him, but anything more might be deemed a witch hunt. We can't connect him to a damned thing."

"That might soon change," Al said, "if he has any interest in whatever Victor might be nudging. Can you give me the rest pronto? I need to scoot to my *v... e... t.*"

Victor sighed and turned his head toward Clayton, who stood with arms folded across his chest. "The MO is so varied that's not the issue," Victor said. "We have burglary rings, shoplifting rings, and gangs still trying for the old badger game. The factor that glues all this together is that someone seems to be behind all of them... or most of them, anyway. They get instructions on what might work best for them. Each case reflects on the skills or tendencies they've shown in the past. Almost all have rap sheets, short or some quite a bit longer. They are assured that they will be helped if caught, and so far, almost every bail bondsman in the county has been used. That's the part of the pattern that identifies someone is behind all this, but it doesn't tell us who."

"I've chatted with the sheriffs in the surrounding adjacent counties," Clayton said, "and once I spelled it out, a few said the same might be going on in their backyards."

"This sounds like organized crime," Al said. "Don't you have people focused on that?"

"Still too hazy for them," Victor said. "I'm getting to the point I'd like to hand it over to them. But I can't until I've got a clearer picture, and the whole thing is designed not to let that happen. The lines of communication are too diverse and untraceable, and most of the petty perps caught so far refuse to talk, knowing they'll be on the street in short order."

"You mentioned money drops, where the person behind this gets their cut. Have you—"

Clayton nodded. "Victor tried to get to the person by staking out a spot or two where the cut from the job was to be dropped. He got nothing, and the perps who'd rolled with the info didn't get the usual bail or cheap lawyer either. Word might've gotten out."

"Oh, word got out all right," Victor said. "You know it did. When someone is offering a 'get out of jail' card, that gets known. Petty crime has gone up. But when bail isn't forthcoming because someone finked out, that gets to be common knowledge too."

"Look, can you cut to the chase here? I need to get Tanner to the... you know who."

"Do you mean vet?" Victor asked.

Tanner squirmed and tried to rise.

"Careful. He knows and understands that word."

"Your dog has developed a vocabulary?"

"He grasps a lot of basic, everyday words but has a little trouble with fine distinctions."

"Distinctions like what?"

"Like the difference between *proclivity* and *propensity.*"

Victor sighed and shook his head then went on. "We first got wind of the idea when a few baggage handlers at the airport were exposed by a crackdown. Some didn't even know about each other. If they had, they might not have taken the risks they did. But they all got bailed out and kept their mouths closed. Then we caught a gang heisting semi rigs from truck stops and selling the contents at ten cents on the dollar. Same thing. They were on the streets again that week. Someone is behind this, Al, and the regular guys we would look to, like this Kemper Giles, seem as puzzled and wary as we are."

Al looked at Clayton.

"Something's sure enough not right here," the sheriff said.

"What do you mean?" Al asked.

"You know that feeling you get when you put your shorts on backward?"

"Well... um... I suppose."

"It's like that."

"But why me? Why bother to fill me in on this? All I want to do is get my dog checked and go home, possibly get on the lake before sundown. This still sounds like a bucket of loose ends. Are these guys more clever than we think, or are they the idiots we think they are, who have been duped and have no way of getting themselves off the hook?"

"I'll admit the paint's still a bit damp"—Clayton glanced toward where the department's animal control truck was heading back out the lane—"too much so for me to dedicate much more time and energy than I have already."

"I'll agree there," Al said.

Clayton nodded. "You see, as matter of fact, I think Victor is having one of those wild-hair ideas like you used to get. He thinks a mastermind is behind all this, one smart enough to know how to sail under the radar and not get noticed."

"But Victor noticed."

"He's a bit like you were when you were young."

"You saying I'm not young?"

"You and I both have mirrors. Don't start in on that."

"But you and Victor think there's some sort of Professor Moriarty behind what looks, on the face of it, to be minor crime after minor crime?"

"Was it a minor crime when they stole your dog?" Victor asked.

"Touché."

"What do you want from me?"

"My original intention in coming out here was to ask you to back off, to avoid getting involved in this. But I can see that, with a hurt dog, you're already half-cocked and on the prod about this."

"You don't think there's anything behind Victor's idea?"

"I won't go so far as to call it cockamamie, but I will say it seems a little far-fetched."

"I'll tell you this: I intend to find whoever is behind hurting Tanner, and if it turns out to be some puppeteer in the wings, I'd like to expose him and give him a public spanking or whatever he deserves."

"I feared as much," Clayton said. "Well, if you're all fired up and committed, I at least want you to help Victor, give him a boost."

"On an official basis?"

"No."

"Semiofficial?"

"No."

"Are you at least going to pay my vet bill?"

"Is it likely to be a stiff one?"

"Probably."

"Then no."

Al shook his head. "Then why okay me helping Victor?"

"As soon as I heard you were on this scene, I figured you'd be working up some wild hair about leaping in. We were liable to find you sticking your nose into this anyway. You've already had a visit from Dom Strobinsky, which means you're a person of interest to someone. And, most of all, because we'd rather know what you're doing than guess."

WHEN AL PULLED INTO his lane and started back toward his house, he saw a long black car parked in front.

"Didn't someone just mention something about Dom being picked up from the prison by a limo?" Maury asked. He held Tanner on his lap.

"Indeed they did." Al's lips tightened into a line. "Indeed they did," he repeated through clenched teeth.

Chapter Three

Al pulled his truck up behind the new black Cadillac XTS limousine until his truck's bumper nearly touched the limo's back bumper.

Fergie and Bonnie were standing between the house and the limo. Fergie was once again holding her Glock down at her side. Bonnie's arms were folded across her chest, her Smith & Wesson Chief's Special visible in her right hand.

As Al got out of his truck and lowered Tanner to the ground, the third and back doors of the limo opened on the right, the side nearer the house. When Al went around the back of his truck, he handed the leash to Maury, who led the dog toward the house.

Tanner was only limping slightly, but three of his legs and one spot on his rump were covered with white gauze and tape where the vet had shaved away some fur and treated the abrasions.

"Oh my gosh," Bonnie said. "What happened to Tanner?"

"He got tossed out of a moving car," Maury said. "At least no bones were broken, and the doc said she didn't think he had internal injuries. He's a tough old fellow."

He paused to let Fergie and Bonnie each pet Tanner on the head before leading him to the front door. But he didn't put the dog indoors. Maury stood there instead, as if waiting to see whether he or Tanner would be needed outside.

Al stayed fixed on the man standing beside the limo. Kemper Giles wore what looked like a dark pin-striped Armani Collezioni suit over an open-collared black dress shirt. The shoes looked like Gucci from where Al stood, though he was no expert. For a landscaper, Kemper was way overdressed, and he looked too slick and slimy to be a funeral director.

He held out a hand, which Al ignored. Then he waved toward the women. "Tell them I'm okay, that they can trust me."

"I will when I believe that," Al said.

"You know," Kemper said, nodding toward the two women, "it's probably illegal for those gals to be waving those guns around in a threatening manner like that."

"Make the call," Al said. "We'll see how it goes."

Maury held Tanner's leash. He looked at Al but said nothing.

"Can we just talk?" Kemper asked.

"About what?"

"Someone's hurting my business. I want to find out who."

"What are they doing? Are they stealing your grass seeds or unplanting your trees?"

"It's not about the landscaping, per se."

"I didn't think so."

The limo's driver, Dom, got out on the driver's side. He just stood there, letting his black suit jacket hang open to show he carried no gun, which wouldn't have gone well for an ex-con. He wore a white shirt with a narrow black tie. At least he hadn't been made to wear one of those dorky chauffeur caps. His face was wrestling with trying to look threatening and a little embarrassed at the same time.

"Will you at least consider it?"

"No."

"Why?"

"I work for a certain sort of clientele."

"You don't think I'm wealthy enough?" Kemper couldn't help himself and glanced over at his limo.

"On the contrary. I work most often for folks on the other end of the spectrum, those who tend to be bowled over by the rich and would-be powerful."

Dom gave Kemper a sort of "I told you so" look. Without another word, the two men got back into the limo, and it pulled away, its engine making little more noise than a mouse yawning, only a low hum.

"That went well," Fergie said.

"About as expected," Al said.

"Is he dangerous?"

Al shrugged. "There's just something about him. He reminds me of that fellow who was working on a building site in a big city. The construction manager suspected him of stealing but could never catch him. Each time the guy would leave the site with a pile of straw in his wheelbarrow, the manager would dig through the straw but found nothing. Finally, on the last day of construction, the manager said to the guy, 'Look, I know you're stealing something. I'm not going to do anything to you now, but tell me what you're stealing.' The worker gave him the same smarmy smile this Giles fellow wears and said, 'Wheelbarrows.'"

Fergie's lips twisted to one side.

"Now, I want to make sure that Tanner gets comfortable after the day he's had," Al said.

"And I have to check on Little Al." Bonnie shoved her stubby pistol inside her belt so that her round little belly pressed against it.

Maury handed Tanner's leash to Al and opened the front door for the ladies. Once inside, Al unhooked Tanner's leash. The dog trotted over to the couch with only the slightest of limps and jumped up into his favorite spot in the corner. He began licking his paws, something he'd done diligently, even a little obsessively, since Al had gotten him from that rescue center.

"We haven't heard the last of him, have we?" Fergie put her pistol on the kitchen counter where she could get at it easily, then she started a fresh pot of coffee.

Al shook his head. "Or others like him." Bonnie went to put her gun away, and Maury followed her down the stairs, probably to make sure Little Al was still sleeping in his crib.

Fergie nodded toward the splashes of white gauze on Tanner's legs. "He sure looks like he's been to the wars." She poured coffee into two mugs.

"The vet said no bones were broken," Al said. "He's just scuffed up in a few places. But he won't be playing the piano for a few days."

"If we had a piano," Fergie said.

Al sat beside Tanner on the couch.

Fergie brought over his steaming mug and put it on the coffee table, where he could reach it.

Al reached over to pet Tanner, smoothing over some ruffled spots in his fur and getting to those spots behind Tanner's ears while he was at it.

Tanner turned his head and licked along the back of Al's hand and thumb. Al turned the hand so Tanner could lick the palm. The palm licking was a fairly new thing, something the dog hadn't done right out of the rescue center. At first, Al had pulled his hand away, but he'd learned to leave the hand there and let Tanner lick it as if it was Al's paw. He'd thought about it and realized that was all the dog had to give back.

"I think he's thanking you," Fergie said.

Al nodded. "He's probably especially thankful after his day of being rolled like a soccer ball into a roadside ditch."

"What did you do to the dognappers when you caught up to them?"

"Nothing. Victor Kahlon and a few other deputies were on hand to keep me from sorting those two out."

"Just as well. You sort hard."

He lifted his mug off the coffee table with the hand not petting Tanner and took a careful sip. He looked over the rim at Fergie.

"What fresh new hell are we in for this time?" she asked.

"You haven't mentioned anything about a wedding. I did sort of propose to you a while back."

"Yeah, you sort of did."

"And?" he asked.

"We never seem to get around to talking about it. Something always comes up."

As she spoke, three rifle shots slammed into the house, breaking glass in the floor below.

Her eyes opened wide then narrowed to angry squints just before Al pushed her down onto the floor.

Tanner shot up and raced, bandages and all, to the screen door leading to the porch overlooking the lake, and he began barking.

Al went over to the doorway, slid the screen to one side, and eased out onto the porch. A boat was turning and heading away. At least it wasn't the same cigarette boat from earlier.

Tanner had all four legs planted at the edge of the porch, and had it not been for the railing, he might have jumped off to the ground a floor below to chase after the departing boat.

"We need to check downstairs," Al called out to Fergie.

She was already heading down.

Maury was at the back of the downstairs room, bent over as he sheltered Bonnie, who was bent over Little Al's crib. Even in the chaos of the moment, Al felt a surge of pride that Maury's first instinct had been to protect his wife and child. He could recall a time when Maury would have dived under the queen-sized bed and let everyone else take care of themselves.

Glass had shattered out of three of the small panes of glass forming a bigger picture window looking out over the lake. Bright shards of broken glass glittered in piles on the red-carpeted floor. Three holes dotted the wall above where Maury and his family were huddled.

Fergie noticed how high the bullet holes were too. "Do you think that was just a warning?"

Al nodded, but heat still warmed his face as the anger inside him boiled into a roil of wanting to take action. But he stopped himself.

Fergie watched him closely. "Let me guess at the Al Quinn thought process here. Your very first notion was to hop into your truck to chase after Kemper Giles. Your second was to fire up your boat and race after that boat, knowing you couldn't catch it, however fast your bass boat is. That's aside from it being in the middle of getting its bilge pumps replaced. Now, I'm waiting for the dime to drop on Plan C."

Al tugged his cell phone out and punched in the number for Victor Kahlon. When Victor answered, Al said, "Victor, could you do me a favor and have your guys on the lake see if a blue-on-white Sea Ray shows up abandoned at one of the south-shore boat ramps on Lake Travis?"

"Dare I ask why?"

"Someone just shot at my house."

"Okay. I'll make a few calls and get back to you."

"What are we going to do?" Bonnie asked as Al slipped his phone back into his pocket. "Take off again and hide somewhere like we've done before?"

"The sheriff hasn't gotten a new trailer yet, has he?" Maury asked. "Like the one we hid in the last time, the one that got burned down."

"Fond memories for him. No, he hasn't." Al glanced toward Fergie, whose mouth twisted sourly.

"Whoever is behind this seems to have very good intel," Al said. "He's invasive and insidious as well as someone we can't deal with by hiding."

"He must have a soul of raw evil for you to truck out the fifty-cent words." Bonnie clutched Little Al closer to her chest.

His face barely poked out of the soft blanket wrapped around him. At least he seemed to be making the most he could of a bad situation. His eyes were closed, and he looked contented.

"What I think you're describing, despite saying nothing specific at all, is nothing less than domestic terrorism," Fergie said.

Al nodded. "If the someone knows as much as it seems he does, he could find Maury and Bonnie if they hid. Or if I put the boat up in dry dock until this is over, he could find it and burn it, just to make a point. We're as exposed as we've ever been. It's also what makes me think Kemper Giles isn't the one behind this, no matter what sort of pond scum he is."

Al figured Kemper was as scared as he was. As much as he hated to admit it, Al was feeling that familiar tingle that made him look behind every bush he passed and keep an eye out in all directions. He'd faced fear before, and that was how he always responded to it—taking it on. He didn't care for it, not a tiny bit... but he damn sure wasn't going to let it get the best of him.

He glanced toward where Fergie was sweeping shards of broken glass into a dustpan. She nodded without him having to say a word.

Al started clearing out the frames of the broken windows. He would pick up more panes and have them puttied into place before the day was over. Maury came back into the downstairs room, carrying an empty pizza box and a couple other empty cardboard boxes Al could cut to cover the holes until he got back with the panes.

"We all start carrying," Al said, "from now on. Maury, I'll get the Model Twelve Winchester out of the gun safe for you. You know how to use it, and though it's only a twelve gauge, it'll do for anything close."

The same went for Bonnie's peashooter, her .38 Chief's Special—a belly gun at best, though her pappy had raised her to be a crack shot with just about any firearm.

"And you, Al?" Fergie asked.

"I'm going to fix the windows then get the boat together and ready to run if we need it. And I'm going to have a pistol and maybe a long gun with me as I do it."

"It sounds like we're at war," Bonnie said.

"We are," Fergie said.

Al's phone rang. He answered when he saw the call was from Victor.

"Found the boat," Victor said. "It's been wiped clean of any prints. Want to catch me up on your end?"

"I dug a couple of the bullets out of the wall. I can get them to you for checking. But just at eyeball glance, I'd say they were from a .270. Not the 5.8-to-7.1-gram ones or the 9.1 to 10.4 ones for bigger game, but the 8.4-gram ones used around here for deer hunting, and deer poaching for all that. Might even be one of those new low-drag bullets that allow for longer range. The boat was quite a ways from the house."

"You got that from an eyeball glance?" Fergie muttered.

Al held a hand over his phone, a sign for her to wait.

"Any thoughts?" Victor asked.

"You mean is it tied to the sort of thing you were looking into? Hard to tell. But it's one damned helluva coincidence if it isn't."

"I called the boat's owner. He's heading over to the ramp to pick it up, and he's madder than forty dozen wet hens." Victor paused. "Do you think it was just a warning?"

"I think we need to find our shooter."

"Anyone come to mind on that side of the lake who's been up for poaching before?" Victor asked.

"Buddy Joe Swanson and his poaching pal, Ferman Laham, come to mind."

"You think they'd rise to the challenge of someone offering them money to do something harebrained like this? Especially if they thought they had no chance of getting caught?"

"Without hesitation."

"I believe I'll pay them a visit," Al said.

"I'd better be with you when you do—you know, make it official and all."

Chapter Four

Fergie leaned against the side of his truck, her elbows on the sill of his open window. The truck was running, the engine rumbling low, like a beast ready to leap into the fray. But it was Fergie, so Al waited, eager though he was to meet up with Victor.

"What do you think is going on?" she asked.

"I'm nowhere near any conclusions or deductions. I'm still gathering and thinking. You know how I work. It's all a dark void until some or all of this starts to make any sense."

"I'll bet Victor even said he could take care of things on the other side of the lake, that you didn't need to go."

"You take care of yourself and the others here," Al said. "I'll be back."

"He probably thinks you'd pound the eyebrows off those poachers for shooting at your home and family."

"He's not altogether wrong."

"Do you think you're being paranoid?"

"Sometimes, paranoia is just having all the facts."

"You don't have any facts."

"Same thing."

One of her eyebrows arched in a way he'd never been able to achieve, even after considerable practice in front of a mirror. "Oh, go on." She pushed at his shoulder. "Just come back. Please?"

She stood waving as he pulled away. He didn't need to be able to see her face to know it wasn't her happy face.

As he drove his truck the long way around the lake to meet up with Victor halfway, he mulled over Fergie's lot. Waiting was a horrible

29

thing. Doing nothing was far worse than taking action. He would've asked her to come along, but she could help more at the house if Bonnie, Maury, Little Al, and Tanner were threatened.

Victor was waiting for him beside the first of two sheriff's department cruisers parked at a former Circle C convenience store that had been converted into a mom-and-pop gas station and general store. In that case, Al knew the mom and pop. They were a couple named Ferguson in their late thirties. He'd helped them when they'd been robbed right after opening. They'd told him he could park his truck behind their building. Once he locked the truck, he followed Victor over to the second waiting cruiser. Two wide-eyed, fresh-cheeked young deputies were sitting inside.

Al's first thought was to ask Victor if those two even shaved yet. They looked right out of high school to Al. But that was the way of most things ever since he'd retired.

"I was just telling these guys that you were the one who arrested Buddy Joe Swanson and Ferman Laham the last time," Victor said. "Those two should be real happy to see you."

Al glanced in at the deputies. "The fish-and-wildlife folks ended up pressing the charges against them. I'd just done the tracking-down-and-nabbing part. And no, they weren't tickled puce or any other color to see me then. I doubt if they'll be doing sideways cartwheels about it this time."

The two deputies nodded, almost in perfect unison. They were both trying very hard to look serious and tough. That usually worried Al. He glanced toward Victor but didn't ask if this was an early outing for the two deputies. They looked like pissed-off boy scouts. He shrugged to himself and said nothing, following Victor over to the lead cruiser.

They rode silently for the next fifteen miles until Victor turned off the two-lane road onto a twin-rut dirt lane leading back to a hovel of a cottage.

Halfway back the lane, each fence post had a catfish head nailed to it, good-sized ones, shown for local bragging rights, no matter how they'd been caught. The men they were calling on had been busted for illegal trotlines a couple of times before. Al had come across a whole stretch of shoreline a quarter of a mile long with illegal lines running from the shore out into the water. To be legal, trotlines had to be run from floats, and each had to have the name and address of the person who'd put the lines out. The ones he'd come across were as illegal as it got. So he drifted along the entire stretch and cut every line, knowing that probably cost someone plenty for that much gear. He'd only wished he could be at the spot when they came back and found their effort and money wasted.

Victor pulled the cruiser up until its front bump guard was almost touching the grill of an ancient, rusting red Ford Ranger parked in front of the only building at the back of the lane.

Victor spoke to the two climbing out of the other car. "Keep in mind that these two are apt to be as slippery as lubricated eels. They would rather run than stand and fight and would rather hide than be found at all. Where'd you get them the last time, Al?"

"Cowering in a dumpster."

"But that doesn't mean they won't shoot you," Victor said, "if they have a clear shot at your back when you can't see them."

Al caught their glances to each other. *Hotshots.* Victor must've seemed like an old man to them, and Al would be positively Stone Age. *Man, they're eager.* One already had a hand down on his sidearm and was holding back a grin.

Whoa. Hold on there a minute, Al. You were sure fire enough of a hothead yourself back in the day. It took almost thirty years of every kind of experience to knock most of the burrs off that attitude, and it's still not all gone.

"Remember," Victor said, "we don't have a warrant at this point. So easy does it."

Al climbed out of the cruiser, and Victor waved a hand for him to wait. The younger two were still glancing at each other as they followed Victor to the front door.

Wind and weather had sanded most of the olive-green paint off the cottage, leaving wood that looked silver and warped here and there.

All three of the uniformed deputies went to the front door, then one of the younger ones slipped around toward the back door just as Victor began pounding on the door.

"Sheriff's Department," he said. "Open up."

Al eased away from the cruiser and sidled over until he could look down the side of the cottage, where a frosted window sat high up one paint-chipped wall—probably the bathroom. He watched as the bottom pane slid up and a foot started to come out.

"Victor!" Al yelled.

By that time, Buddy Joe Swanson was all the way out the window and had dropped to the ground. His hands were empty. He saw Al and took off running.

Al had the angle on him and ran fast enough to cut off Swanson's run. He leaped in a flying tackle and pulled the flailing ankles together.

Swanson's body slapped the ground with a thud. "Police brutality!" he yelled. "Police brutality. He hit me. Did everyone see he hit me?"

"Pipe down," Al said.

One sleeve of Swanson's black hoodie had pulled up his arm far enough to expose a tattoo that proclaimed, "All you need is a hoodie and a woodie."

His teeth bared when he looked up at Al. "Aw, man, it's you."

"Indeed it is."

Al had one arm twisted up behind Swanson's back by the time the other three deputies came running around to that side of the house, two of them with sour looks.

One of the younger deputies had his gun out. The other held a taser.

"If you tase him while I'm holding him, you are going to be power-fully sorry!" Al shouted.

Victor gave them a look. They holstered their toys and leaped onto the two on the ground.

"Give me your hands. Give me your hands!" one of them yelled as he wrestled with Swanson.

Al had had control of Swanson, but these two seemed to like to start over. Al let go of him. As soon as one of the younger ones had a cuff on one wrist, Al struggled to get up and out of the way. He could tell he was spoiling the party for the newer deputies.

"The other one!" Al shouted as he struggled to his feet. "Did you check for the other one?"

Victor spun and ran toward the front of the house.

Al watched a foot start out of the bathroom exit Swanson had tak-en. Ferman Laham landed on the ground beneath the open bathroom window. He took off running like a rabid coyote with its tail on fire. Al ran after him. Unfortunately for Laham, Victor was just coming back around the corner of the house, and the two only avoided colliding because Laham swerved, swept around him, and took off toward the truck.

The two younger deputies left Swanson on the ground and took off after Laham. Both had twenty to thirty pounds of gun belt and other gear on, but they outran their quarry while he was still trying to yank open the truck door and climb inside.

Swanson tried to struggle to his feet despite wearing handcuffs. Al stepped closer and put a foot on Swanson's chest, holding him to the ground.

"Ow. Yer killin' me. Call an ambulance!"

Swanson was not going gently into that good night. Al glanced to-ward Victor, who was grinning back.

"So it was just the two of you in that boat?" Al asked.

"What boat?"

"The one you used to shoot at my house."

"I don' know where you live. I don' even go over ta that side o' the lake."

Victor shook his head, fighting to keep from laughing out loud. "How do you know where Al lives?"

"I... I just do. Everyone does."

"I doubt that," Victor said.

When they stood him up, Swanson tried to shake loose and ended glaring at Victor and Al. "I'll be back on the street by this afternoon. Gotta, you know. My girlfriend's getting out of prison. I'll be out an' waitin' on her." He wore a red-black-and-white-checked flannel shirt, cut off at the shoulders. His jeans had large holes at each knee, and not to make a fashion statement. Somewhere in the scuffle of being tackled and held down, both of his elbows had been scuffed and were lightly bleeding. His unwashed hair hung to his shoulders, having come loose from a man bun. His chin and cheeks were covered with uneven patches of black stubble. He should've looked subdued but didn't. Instead, he seemed cocky, as though he knew someone had his back.

Al was glad they'd at least stopped the two of them before they got to the truck. Although television chase scenes usually show cops getting their man by outrunning him or using spike strips, Al knew the culprit did get away about a third of the time, most often because the cops on the chase or their superiors had decided not to endanger innocent people who happened to be on the roads.

The two deputies loaded Laham into the back of their cruiser and came back for Swanson. They looked just a bit sheepish for having taken off, leaving him in the care of someone like Al.

"This afternoon. I'll be walking tall and free. You'll see." Swanson tried to swagger as he was led toward the back seat of the second cruiser.

Al had turned to Victor but heard Swanson spit. Then he heard a slap. By the time he turned his head, Swanson's lower lip was bleeding from a split in the middle. He tried to spit again, but before he could, one of the deputies held him still while the other slipped a spit mask over Swanson's head. He could see and breathe through the gauzy mask, but any more spit would get only on himself.

"Who hired you to shoot at Al's house?" Victor asked before they loaded him in with Laham.

"I ain't a-sayin' nothin.'" Not quite true to his word, he didn't say anything else while being loaded into the cruiser, except for a string of cussing that contained nothing Al hadn't heard before.

The backup cruiser headed out the lane, roiling up another brown cloud of dust, taking their two passengers to jail for evading and resisting even if nothing else stood.

"If those two were right about their situation, they should be out on bail later in the day," Victor said. "But now that those fresh deputies are gone, maybe we can do one or two things I'd prefer they not know about. It's easy to pick up bad habits by example."

"Are we going to take a quick look around inside?" Al was already headed for the front door.

"Of course we are. I'd dearly like to know why these two were pointed toward you."

"So would I."

"More especially, I'd like to know how someone communicates with these sorts of characters."

"None of the ones you've brought in and had to be released shed any light on that?"

"What I got was all over the place. You've got to figure, too, that there are some out there saying no to these offered opportunities. Though they've been more helpful about the methods of approach. With some, it was email; others, text messages; and some got a call or even snail mail. None of it was traceable, even by our tech wizard, Meat Jenkins."

"I can do the snooping around inside on my own," Al said, "if you want deniability."

"What the hell. We crossed the Rubicon when we came out here. Their taking it on the lam out the side window is probable cause enough for me."

Al let Victor lead the way into the dilapidated cottage. The inside looked worse than the outside. What Sheetrock had once graced the walls was broken or worn away for stretches that revealed the two-by-four studs. Two folding cots on opposite sides of the one room made the only sleeping quarters. Al could see no computer or landline phone. The smell of sweaty, dirty clothes was profound enough to hurt Al's eyes. Victor was blinking as well. One corner of the cabin was dedicated to a shower stall with a toilet in it, a multipurpose place with no privacy. These fellows were sure living la dolce vita.

Victor bent to reach under one of the cots and lifted a Winchester .270 semiautomatic rifle with a scope. "Same gun Buddy Joe used to poach deer, I'm betting. He at least should have used another weapon, one we don't already have a ballistics sample of. We might be able to hold them a day or two longer than they expect, which could give us a chance to lean on them a bit. I suspect Laham, the rabbit, will prove to be the weaker link."

"One thing niggles," Al said. "Do the people being recruited, or used, usually come in twos?"

"Nope. Sometimes three, four, or more are involved. Other times, it's just one person with certain lowlife skills."

"But the incentives and promises of help getting out of jail if caught are the same?"

"Those vary too."

"Still, no one knows anything?"

Al's eyes were still stinging just from being inside the cottage—a ripe mix of ammonia, stale dust, and sweat. He couldn't spot anything else they could use to backtrack to anyone behind the actions of the two. "Do you think one person is behind this or more?"

"I don't know."

"Still, what you're describing hints at a Professor Moriarty type—someone manipulating people, lots of them, for a profit."

"Maybe. Although Clayton is no fan of that theory. In fact, he called it a notion and a somewhat sucky one at that."

"His words?"

"I embellished and toned down his version." Victor looked around the room one last time then started for the door. "But he did say that he often gave you slack on such wild fancies, and you came through frequently enough."

Once outside again, Al took a deep breath of air. "One person, eh, pulling the puppet strings of characters like these two?" He shook his head.

"I said I don't know the number or gender of anyone behind all this, but there does seem to be some concerted orchestration by at least one person."

"Let me suggest one thing I learned from a singer-songwriter friend of mine," Al said.

"Do tell." Victor stopped to listen, holding the rifle down at his side in one hand.

"The guy I'm talking about was working his way up and really seemed to be going places. Then it all stopped."

"What happened?"

"He met a loving woman."

"How did that—"

"You see, his songs before were full of angst, the sort of misery of the soul with which much of his audience could relate. You know: broken heart and lost love. But when he became happy, that went away. It's not that his music was all daisies popping out of his ass, but the bitterness in his twang eased up. His crowd felt less that mattered deeply to them."

"How's that apply here?"

"I think whoever is behind this is someone not at the top of his or her game, someone who's still struggling to come out on top. But there's a sure enough fire in the belly, enough to risk this sort of arm's-length dabbling in crime. He's far from being content or comfortable."

Victor nodded. "Plus, the person probably wants to make money while feeling safe doing so."

While he drove Al back to his truck, Victor glanced over at him. "You look disappointed."

"I would have liked to have uncovered the tiniest thread about who's behind the antics of guys like this, especially since their paid assignment seems to have been to shoot at my house."

"Keep in mind that Clayton thinks the whole idea is slightly preposterous, but most of the ones involved, who I've talked to, stay dead silent. The few I do get to talk have little of value to share. That aspect is what first got me thinking something bigger was going on behind a lot of petty crimes. This is a pretty well-thought-out and orchestrated scheme. For every one I talk to, there could be ten to a hundred more out there, each turning their tiny share of money over to whoever is behind this. It may be petty stuff, but the scale could be huge, and it must have been going on for a while to fund the anonymous bail bonding and lawyers hired for the few caught while countless others keep pillaging on."

"You're getting nothing from the lawyers or bail people?"

"Most are a carefully picked lot glad to be getting steady incomes from this sort of thing. The rest stand on lawyer-client privilege and head to the bank with what's in their pockets. You've seen at least one of them in those television commercials where he stands with clenched fists and tells miscreants that they're safe with him because he doesn't take any lip from 'the man.'"

"Frustrating, eh?" Al watched a hillside covered in mountain cedar go by outside his window. "I imagine that's why the regular big-time outfits are getting annoyed by the very vagueness but effectiveness of this, at least to the extent I got somehow swept up in whatever the hell is going on."

At the convenience store, Al climbed into his truck and headed back to his house as fast as he could legally go, eager to keep everyone close to him secure from a force that, so far, seemed invisible and perhaps untouchable.

On his hurried way home, left to his own thoughts, he had time to fret once again about what to do to protect the family he'd never expected to have. He could hardly load them up in vehicles and send them scurrying around like gypsies on the run. But then again, it could come to that.

The thing about guys like Swanson and Laham, the toe-jam sort that could be hired for very little to do all kinds of damage or commit any number of crimes, was that they filled all the darkest corners of a county like his, as well as the surrounding ones. Al thought it likely, even probable, that one could be hired to sneak up to his house with a can of gas. His insides crawled with the tension of having to do something once again but not even knowing what would be most effective. He might be able to protect his so-called family, but he could lose his house or boat just because someone wanted to send a message, one that wouldn't make him stop anyway but would just fire him up to find the manipulator. He caught himself pressing harder on the accelerator.

He slowed when a roadrunner strutted across the road ahead of him.

He'd always considered roadrunners good luck. They seemed to mind their own business and cleaned up snakes and such. They didn't fly but sure got around, and they could even hop up into and climb trees. A bookstore-owning pal of his, Vonnie, once told him she'd witnessed one go right up a slanting tree trunk and eat the baby blue jays out of a nest like popcorn. But he supposed it was a bird-eat-bird world out there at times.

He didn't see any reason to read the sighting like an omen, so he stuck with the good-luck part and drove on.

Chapter Five

Eager to get back to his house pronto, Al caught himself going faster than he should a couple of times. His foot kept wanting to press down harder on the accelerator. He gave himself a "Whoa, Nellie" and forced himself to go slow and steady enough to look into the brush on either side of the two-lane road leading to his drive. He drove past his lane and kept looking. *Nothing.* He didn't spot any vehicles parked too close or see any hint of where one might have been driven into thicker brush and hidden.

He sighed and took out his phone as he headed back to his lane.

Fergie answered at the first ring. "Where are you?"

"Just coming in the lane. I had a look around. Where is everyone?"

"Well, Maury's in the house with the baby in a papoose carrier. He's got your shotgun."

At least Maury knew how to use it, while he had none of Bonnie's country-raised skills with handguns.

"Bonnie's up on the sniper roost where that guy tried to get a bead on the house once before, and she made him sorry for it. She has your thirty-ought-six," Fergie said. "With that scoped rifle of yours, she claims she could shoot the eyelashes off a flea from up there."

"And you?"

"I'm down on the boat dock. They came that way before. We're on full alert here now that you seem to have a nemesis."

"Fergie?"

"Yeah?"

"You know how you're always saying it's good for a man to show vulnerability at times? Well, I can't say I care for it when that vulnerability extends to my house and the people in it."

"I hear you. I'll be headed up to the house for a family meeting."

The rest of the way up the lane, he paid special attention to the surrounding wooded areas. The trees and underbrush had grown thick because he'd let them so that the dense green could act as a buffer. He'd often kept a sharp eye out for the subtle movement of deer masked in the underbrush while he walked Tanner. Sometimes, he'd even seen them move away while the dog was busy sniffing the ground.

The influx of new homes and more people had crowded the land that had once been a free place for critters of all kinds to roam. He'd fed and watered the deer through the drought years and felt some of their angst as they moved on their way through far less wilderness.

He parked in front of his door and was tempted to leave his truck running. Fergie's car was already loaded and poised to go. A suitcase stuck up in the back seat above other stuff.

When Al headed inside, Tanner rushed up. Bandages and all, he seemed ready for action in the home-defense effort.

Maury, with the shotgun leaning in a corner and Little Al in the papoose holder on his chest, was gathering up dog food and bowls. "I just remembered we needed to pack for Tanner as well."

Fergie came in the front door. "I took a look all around the house once as I came up the hill." She nodded to Maury. "You're sure getting into the spirit of being prepared."

He grinned back. "You know, it's like how you should brush your teeth anyway, not just because you might get into a spur-of-the-moment French-kissing session with some stranger."

"Really, Maury?" Al shook his head.

"I'm just glad Bonnie wasn't down from her perch yet to hear that," Fergie said.

As if on cue, Fergie's phone rang. She listened, whispered something back, and put the phone back in her pocket. "Bonnie's spotted something."

"What?"

"She doesn't know. She had a glimmer of movement, but it's stopped."

"Maury, you stay here." Al hurried to his bedside nightstand and got out his backup Glock. His Sig Sauer was already in the truck's glove box.

Fergie had tucked her Glock into her jeans at the small of her back. Al nodded to her, and they slipped out the front door. Al had to use the side of his foot to keep Tanner from following them outside. He seemed eager for the hunt, while Al felt the usual flutter of edgy tension of being prepared for gunfire.

They hurried at first then slowed to pick their steps carefully so as not to break a twig or rustle leaves. He hadn't asked where Bonnie had seen movement, but Fergie pointed two fingers at her own eyes then indicated to the left.

In another ten yards, Al held up a hand for Fergie to slow. He'd caught a glimpse of something. Al moved as quietly as he could, in stealth mode, until he'd eased close enough to see clearly. He stood from his crouch and waved for Fergie to come up beside him. Ahead, a woman was tied to the trunk of a live oak tree. A red gas can sat beside her on the ground.

The woman shook her head when she saw Al.

"Does that woman know you?" Fergie asked.

"Not in the biblical sense. But I arrested her a time or two. Her preferred AKA is Dolores del Rio."

"Really? Wasn't that a Mexican film actress from back in Orson Welles's day?"

"Yeah, but we'll get more out of her if we meet her in the middle and do it her way."

"Okay. Dolores it is. How do you suppose she ended up tied to that tree?"

"I suppose we should go ask her."

"Before we do, what did you arrest her for?"

"Arson. She's kind of a special-needs, high-maintenance sort of gal. She wanted to be supported but couldn't get along with any man. So she turned her business sense to setting things on fire for a price."

"Arsonists are among the hardest to catch," Fergie said. "They can be long gone before the fire department even shows."

"That's what tripped up Dolores. She had torched three fireworks stands in a row, just for the fun of it, apparently. Someone spotted her across a road from one fire where cartwheels and Roman candles were still shooting every which way. She might have gotten away, but she couldn't stop giggling. I just scooped her up. She was still letting out chuckles all the way in to be booked."

"Hey, Mr. Dinkhead detective. You gonna come cut me loose, or what?"

"Coming, Dolores." Al gave Fergie an eye roll and lowered his voice. "Remember, she might just share a thing or two if we respect her enough to stick with calling her Dolores."

"That's what that woman is screaming for, respect, tied up to a tree in the woods that way."

Al made a quick call on his phone.

Victor Kahlon sounded snappish. "What now?"

"Dolores del Rio. On my property. She has a can of gas. I'm going to see if I can get a lead from her." He hung up, knowing that Victor might grouse but would be heading Al's way in moments.

As Al neared the tree, he could see Dolores had been tied awfully well. A pocketknife had been taken from her and lay on the ground next to the gas can.

She was as slim as a stick of jerky, with skin tanned a dark brown by many hours outside, as shiny and hard looking as flint. Her outfit was a denim shirt over worn blue jeans and Red Wing boots.

A piece of paper was pinned to the front of her blouse. When he was close enough, Al could make out the block-printed letters: "Your welcome. Dom."

Al could have faulted the lug's grammar, but what was sending a rush of heat up to his face was the guy's presence. He leaned closer to Fergie and whispered, "If the intel of these guys is good enough to know someone is coming after me, why can't they find out who the guy behind this is?"

She shook her head.

"Who sent you to do this, Dolores?" Al asked.

"You know I can't say. In this case, I couldn't even if I was so disposed, or inclined, which I ain't."

"How did you hear about the job?"

"Wouldn't you like to know?"

"I would."

"Well, you can just sit on that wish and spin. Now, untie me."

"Nope." Al started toward her.

Fergie put a hand on his shoulder. "Let me take a stab at this. I suspect your opportunity to be good cop passed some time ago."

Al moved away while Fergie went to stand beside Dolores.

"Ya gonna undo me? I'm trussed up like a turkey here."

"You know I can't do that," Fergie said. "It's a shame you let someone dupe you this way."

"No one dupes me. Never."

"Well, they've got you headed for jail."

"Not for long. I'll be out before tomorrow morning's sparrow farts."

A sheriff's department cruiser was coming up Al's lane. He moved away from the delightful conversation to meet with Victor, who was behind the wheel.

As soon as Victor spotted Al coming through the woods, he slowed to a stop and stepped out of the cruiser, stretching his arms wide and yawning.

"Up all night?" Al asked.

"You know how it is. Where is she?" He peered past Al's shoulder.

"Back yonder, tied to a tree by Dom. He or his boss, Kemper Giles, thinks he's my protector now."

"Well, crap. How do you feel about that?"

"I'd just as soon see Giles in jail as not. But if all these petty little crimes are biting into any of his revenue streams, that at least makes this mess more interesting. I'm not at all comfortable, though, with being on the same side as his sort of pond scum. I damn sure don't want him as my protector."

"But if he is," Fergie said as she came up to them, "we might be able to stay here at the house until this is solved. It would sure be better than stumbling about through half of Texas on the lam, with your house and boat still at risk."

"There's that," Al agreed.

"You can cuff her and take her away when you want," Fergie told Victor.

"Did you get anything from her?" Victor asked Fergie.

"She said the two big goons looked at her cell phone messages. They probably didn't get much from that. They didn't bother to take the phone to try to track back to the caller."

"Burner phones," Victor said. "The emails aren't much better. I've had Meat Jenkins on it, and he's hit a dead end in every instance."

"You still think someone's pulling the strings on these puppets from somewhere?" Al asked.

"More than ever. You're just lucky I didn't arrive to find you cooking up s'mores over the fire of what was left of your *casa*."

"The text message on her phone was just the usual work-for-hire gig for someone like her," Fergie said.

"Well, with her record, it may be her last for a while."

"The text said she would get sprung from jail, if caught, and provided with a lawyer, if needed."

"Someone has already made a pile of money," Victor said, "and hopes to make piles more with this sort of thing, enough to pay for threatening the likes of you two."

"If they knew Al better, they might think better about riling him," Fergie said.

"That's the way the betting at the department is going," Victor said. "Now, give me a hand getting her cuffed and into the back seat. I'm sure there's a bail bondsman somewhere and yet another one of those ambulance-chasing lawyers all ready to spring into action on her behalf."

"I'd be careful in the handling," Al said. "As I recall, her 'go to' move is biting."

"Duly noted," Victor said.

"At least you won't need a spit mask this time," Al said, "just maybe one of those masks like Hannibal Lector wore."

"Oh," Victor said as they crunched along on fallen leaves, "about a quarter of a mile up the road, I spotted a battered white Ford 150 tucked into some bushes. I ran the plates, and it's hers. I'll have it towed away as well."

Victor started one way with Dolores, and Al and Fergie headed back toward the house. Then they heard a yell.

Al spun and saw Dolores running through the woods in their direction. Despite her hands being cuffed behind her back, she was outrunning Victor.

As she neared, she saw them and veered to her left. Fergie stepped closer and extended one of those long legs of hers. Dolores tripped and

nearly did a midair somersault as she tumbled to the ground and came
to a stop against a prickly agarita bush at the base of a live oak tree.

Dolores struggled to scramble to her feet, but Fergie stepped forward and held her to the ground with one foot.

"Hey, I thought you was on my side," Dolores said.

"Careful. Careful," Fergie said. "Or I'll tell Dom where you live."

He must have put one helluva scare into her while trying to pry information from her because her tanned face washed a shade paler, and
she let them stand her up. Victor held her arm more tightly as he led
her toward his car again.

As Victor's cruiser turned around and headed back out the lane, Al
and Fergie walked back toward the house.

"She went more quietly than I expected," Fergie said.

"I think she's buying into the assurances that she'll be out on the
streets today or tomorrow," Al said. "That's the only thing she would
say, and she said it several times. But I doubt she'll try for the house
again, with the likes of Dom perhaps lurking around. He probably inti-
mated he won't be so nice next time."

"She claims he was particularly graphic in his threats," Fergie said.

"Dom must have chuckled to himself as he was sending us a message when he left her for us to find."

"I'm glad we get to stay at the house," she said.

"I don't care for the conditions, but me too. I imagine Bonnie and
Maury will agree. But it does give me the hotfoot to solve this as soon
as possible."

"And I'll be there to help you, as always," she said.

"I couldn't—or certainly wouldn't—do it without you."

"WELL, WELL, WELL." Fergie stood looking out across Lake Travis while Al wiped his hands on a rag and climbed out of the boat. "I do believe the lake is still capable of peaceful moments now and again."

Al hit a switch that raised the boat into the air in its sling, then he stood beside her and looked across the water. A small breeze kicked up low rows of whitecaps barely above the blue-green surface. An osprey flew by overhead, carrying a midsized bass in its talons, holding the fish head forward and tail back for better aerodynamics.

Times like that moment, even if brief, reminded him why he loved living waterfront on the lake. "At least the bilge pumps are working, though it's too late to head out on the lake now."

Fergie glanced over at the boat. "Do you expect we'll be able to get back to fishing soon and that easygoing life you craved when you retired?"

"You know, I can't really recall too many times lately when I've felt truly retired."

"Feeling a little tension right now?"

He nodded.

"It's always one damned thing or another, isn't it?" She shook her head.

"I just need to find the beginning of any kind of pattern to whatever the hell *is* going on, particularly as it pertains to all of us."

"You're okay with us being able to stay put only because we're under the protection of Kemper Giles and his ex-con posse?"

"Of course not. I don't care for it at all. But it does motivate me to do one thing."

"What's that?"

"To find out exactly how Kemper makes his money. It has to be in a way where the sheer scale of all these petty little crimes eat into his take somehow."

"And you've somehow become an equal enough threat to act upon," she said.

Al heard the growing buzz of a watercraft, not one that was going to go past, but one coming across the lake directly toward them.

"What fresh hell is this?" he asked.

Fergie's eyes opened wide. "I thought we were going to be okay staying put."

"So did I."

As the small dot grew bigger, Al could make out a Jet Ski. Even in the fading light of late afternoon, he could see its sides had a green stripe and it had a solo rider.

As it got closer, the rider slowed and lifted what looked like a rifle.

"Get down!" Al yelled.

Fergie had already dropped to the dock's surface, way ahead of him.

Before the rider could fire, a boat pulled away from the shore a quarter mile up the lake and headed for the Jet Ski. It was no banana boat, but it was big enough to have a couple of 200-hp motors on its transom and was throwing a mighty wake. One person steered the boat, while a second opened fire with a fully automatic weapon.

From the shore to Al's left, more shots were fired. Puffs of water sprays shot up around the Jet Ski where bullets were plowing into the lake.

"I thought Bonnie was up at the house with Maury and the baby," Fergie said.

"She is. That's an AR-15 being fired."

The jet skier had spun and was flat out going as fast as he could, but the boat giving chase was gaining on it as they roared out of sight to the left.

Flashes of blue and red came from the right. A big white sheriff's department boat came zooming in from that direction, lit up with its siren going.

"We certainly live in entertaining times," Fergie said.

Neither of them had tried to rise yet from where they were hugging the boards connecting the boat dock to the fishing dock.

Al wriggled enough to pull his cell phone out of his back pocket and punched in a number.

Victor answered. "You know I'm just about to go off duty, don't you?"

"It's starting to seem like World War Seven out here," Al said.

"I just heard a flutter about that. Clayton has a department boat out doing routine patrols, handily near where you live. Wait. Hold on a minute."

Al glanced at Fergie.

"Is he offering deepest sympathies or anything?" she asked.

Victor came back on. "Okay, Al, the boat giving chase got away, but the Jet Ski rider is in custody. No rifle. He must've tossed it. But they have him for stealing his ride."

"Did you hear anything about someone shooting from the shore-line?"

"They thought that was you."

"Well, it wasn't," Al said.

"We could send a cruiser to nose around from the shore side."

"Naw. I think I know who it might be. Though not a preferred situation, it's probably someone protecting us."

"Some of Kemper Giles's lot?"

"Maybe. I have a hunch that more than his group have a sudden interest in protecting me, if it results in uncovering who's behind all the petty chicanery."

"I have a thought on that you're not going to like," Victor said.

"Can it get more tangled and confusing than it is?"

"It sort of does."

"How so?"

"Our guys on the department boat did catch a glimpse or two of those fellows in the boat protecting your place that chased off the Jet Ski."

"And?"

"One had a distinctive neck tattoo. We think he was in the Aryan Brotherhood."

"Why in the name of Satan's jockstrap would those racist thugs be protecting me?"

"Don't know. But if it's them, they're pretty good at protecting those they want to, and you're not just some other Caucasian in prison."

"Well, I sure as hell don't want their racist help and don't like it."

"But between them and Kemper Giles's thugs, you might be able to focus on helping me with my long shot idea," Victor said. "Just the hint of them being around should strike fear into the hearts of anyone coming at you in the near future. Does this mean you and your tribe won't be heading for the hills?"

"It means I'm going to dig deep and fast to solve this." He glanced toward Fergie. "I mean 'we' are going to get on this, Fergie and me, pronto and with spurs on."

Her frown shifted into an eager, slightly sinister grin.

Chapter Six

Perhaps because she was on the roly-poly side herself, Bonnie had whipped up a breakfast for Al and Fergie that would have staggered a crew of lumberjacks. "Since you're going off to war," she explained, "or at least to fight the good fight."

She had baked a couple of golden Yukon potatoes in the microwave then sliced them thin and fried them with Vidalia onions to go with the two eggs and three rashers of real bacon each though Fergie had tried to switch the household over to turkey bacon a while back. The coffee was rich and hot. Al had two cups of it.

Fergie slipped some of her big breakfast to Tanner, who hovered near enough the table to watch every bite they took. Al should have shared some of his as well instead of eating everything on his plate. As he and Fergie headed out to his truck, he felt as stuffed as a tick, as folks were prone to say in his neck of the woods.

"I doubt we could eat like that often"—Fergie climbed into the passenger seat—"without sooner or later having to be drilled with three holes and turned into bowling balls."

A little over an hour later, Al slowed his truck and spotted Victor Kahlon leaning against the side of a sheriff's department cruiser parked behind two city squad cars. A black Mercedes also sat nearby, probably belonging to a guy in a dark-blue Armani jacket, giving last-second instructions to four city cops.

Al gave a couple of sniffs as he pulled up behind Victor's car.

"It's not the season for cedar fever," Fergie said. "You're not coming down with a cold, are you?"

"No, just remembering. The smells of bacon frying and coffee brewing were sure filling every corner of our place. Someday, I'm going to miss that smell and wish I'd spent more time being bad," Al said.

"We've had this conversation, as I suppose everyone has, who ponders the balance between living a good, careful, and long life against the pleasures of savoring the gusto of a rich life without dwelling on how long it might be. Given all the risks you've taken, I don't even know why you go there."

"As Bonnie put it, 'You all better eat up 'cause ya might just get yourselves shot out there,'" Al said.

Fergie unfastened her seat belt and turned to look at him. "Are you worried?"

"Let's say I'm always carrying around a little cautious edge."

"How do you feel about us all staying at the house?"

"Like the cheese in a mousetrap."

"Don't like it much, eh?"

"Well, at least we're all safe for the moment. Someone, or perhaps a couple of someones, are watching over Maury, Bonnie, the baby, and Tanner, whether they're the kind of people I like or not. It was bad enough with the likes of Dom hovering around. But if those brick-head Aryans are there too..."

"Victor said the department wasn't absolutely sure about that," Fergie said. "All they got was a glimpse of a neck tattoo."

"A mere hint is enough to curdle my cottage cheese."

They shut the truck doors quietly and practically tiptoed over to stand by Victor, who was keeping himself apart from the assault group.

A weathered single-story house with chipping beige paint stood in the dark-green clutter of thick mountain cedars and all kinds of unregulated growth that kept it out of sight from neighboring homes, all equally as rustic. An airplane groaned as it lowered in the sky to approach the airport only a few miles away. The house was technically within the city limits, although the sheriff's department had generated the lead in locating the two men who had warrants outstanding, which was why Victor had been invited, but he'd brought along no other deputies.

He turned to look at Al and Fergie and didn't need to hold a finger to his lips for them to catch the mood. They'd arrived just in time. One member of the assault team carried a small battering ram for the front door, although from what Al could see, he wouldn't need it to bust inside.

The guy in the suit glanced toward them, shared a flicker of a frown, then turned back to the men rushing toward the small house.

"He wears an Armani suit jacket in case the media happens to pop by. Can't miss a moment of publicity," Al whispered into Fergie's ear.

He'd recognized the guy, someone from the District Attorney's office named Cavander Haley. Cav, they called him, and he was the DA's current point guy when it came to organized crime.

She nudged Al with an elbow and pointed at a small tool shed to their right. The door was open half an inch but pulled closed the second Al looked.

Al and Fergie sidled quietly away from Victor and eased toward the shed.

The men, who Al had figured out were from the APD Organized Crime Division's Interdiction Unit, shouted about their warrant and identified themselves as police. Almost without pause, loud thumping began as the front door took two blows before popping open. Two of the men rushed inside while the other two hurried around to the back.

The two guys in the shed took that moment to pop out and break into a run. They caught sight of Al first and chose to veer toward Fergie—big mistake. She stuck out one of her long legs and tripped one. While he was tumbling to the ground in a flurry of brown dust and bits of stunted grass, she was bringing up her right fist from near her right ankle. She caught the second guy in his solar plexus hard enough to lift him off the ground with a loud "Umpf."

Cav spun to look at them. "Hey, out here!" he yelled.

The four cops came pouring out of the house at a run. They crossed the straggly excuse for a yard and piled onto the two near escapees on the ground.

The cop with three stripes on his sleeve looked up at Fergie, who was stepping away. "Ah. Figured that might be you," he said.

Cav knew Al and Fergie too and frowned at Victor when he realized they'd been invited. Still, he couldn't squawk since Fergie had stopped a possible getaway.

He watched as his men in black handcuffed their prizes and loaded them to be hauled away. Cav headed into the weathered green house.

Victor leaned closer to Al and Fergie and whispered, "Meth and coke distribution. These were a couple of small fries I'd seen do a few deals in the county. I'd been hoping to follow them up their ladder, but as soon as Cav got wind that anything organized was going on, he was on this like flies on... well, you know."

One of the unit's men spread a large duffel open outside the front door, and they began to carry out guns, stacks of cash held together with rubber bands, and clear bags of meth and cocaine. One of the men tested some of the meth and nodded to Cav, who was rubbing his hands together as he came over to Victor.

"Are these fellows part of your cockamamie theory, Victor?" He was one of those people who would stand way too close to others, in their space.

If Victor was bothered by Cav's proximity, he didn't show it as he shrugged. "I thought so at first. But they don't match up at all with any of the indicators. You'll notice they didn't go on about getting out of jail like it was a revolving door."

Cav swung his neatly groomed but blockish long head toward Al. "And why's a spent bullet like you tagging along with an active-duty deputy?"

Al took in the suit and wondered if Cav even owned a pair of blue jeans or had ever worn them for a Halloween chuckle. His white shirt was stiff with starch and his tie an aggressive red.

"And if you must know," Cav went on without being asked, "I don't care for Victor's theory that someone is behind and is orchestrating the petty crimes."

"So it's not organized?" Al asked.

"But, Victor," Cav said, "if it turns out you're right, you let me know right away, and I'll take over. That is, the minute you have anything concrete and not just wisps and ideas."

"Why do you think Kemper Giles is fretting about this, then?" Victor asked.

"All you have on Kemper Giles is that he's making more money than he should. And that he somehow feels challenged or threatened by this nemesis figure. If there is one. We're stretched thin with all that's going on and can't dedicate too much time or manpower in that direction."

By "we," he meant the DA, Marshall Asquith III, or "Three" as some called him, though not to his face.

"You're not interested in that hint of the Aryan Brotherhood we got from a boat near Al's house?" Victor asked.

"We are very much interested in the Aryan Brotherhood and their leader, Bitso Mullen, an ex-con who claims to be clean but may have ties to human trafficking. But all you have is a whiff of a rumor from a long-distance sighting. If you get more, you let me know, then get out of the way and let me and my men handle it."

He turned on his heel and headed toward the vehicle loaded with all the evidence taken from the house.

Al shook his head and glanced toward Fergie. Together, they'd seen and experienced about every form of ego, ambition, and politics that being behind the scenes in law enforcement could provide. They had both danced through heavy-handed interactions with state and federal agencies before. Al had always been amazed by how well Sheriff Clayton managed to flex and roll through some pretty sticky moments of uncooperative cooperation. He could tell from Fergie's curled lip she wasn't in a flexible mood.

"Nice guy," she said, letting the sarcasm drip.

"Yeah, a real team player there." Al watched Cav climb into the car and close the door without looking their way. "And he sure didn't think much of your theory, Victor."

Victor shrugged.

Al nodded toward the house. "You think this is some kind of mob or mafia thing?"

"It's enough that Cav thinks it's a link to organized crime," Victor said. "That's all he's focused on these days."

"And the definition for that has broadened in recent years," Fergie said. "They homed in on a group selling bogus tickets to the Austin City Limits concert this year."

"Well, I have other things to do," Victor said, "as I imagine you have as well." He gave a curt wave and headed toward his unmarked car.

As they were climbing back into Al's truck, Fergie said, "That Cav. Did you hear what he called you back there, Al? A spent bullet."

Al shrugged. "That's like being called 'ugly' by a frog."

Chapter Seven

Maury looked up when the front door opened. Bonnie came inside, leading Tanner on a leash. She dropped her end of it, and Tanner rushed over to the couch, where Maury sat holding Little Al.

"Well, are we still not alone out here?" Maury rubbed Tanner behind the ears while Little Al reached out uncertainly to either pet or grab fur.

So far, Tanner had shown himself to be patient and tolerant of the new little person in the house.

"Tanner sniffed out two different spots where folks other than us are guarding the house."

"Isn't that a good thing? Aren't they keeping us safe?"

Bonnie shook her head then started brushing twigs, leaves, and bits of bark off her blouse. "I don't like this. I don't care for it one frog-lick bit."

"What are you thinking?"

"I think we need to skedaddle."

"Al and Fergie are expecting us to stay put."

"So are those guys out there. How long do you think it'll be before they figure out they could use Little Al or you as insurance if they scoop you up?"

"I hadn't thought of that."

"I'll bet *they* have. It's just a matter of time before they act on it. These jaspers are all about controlling the situation... to their advantage."

"Al says he isn't exactly sure how this Kemper Giles fellow makes his money. Neither is anyone else in law enforcement, or they would have moved on it. But the other guy, this Bitso Mullen... They know about him. He's an ex-con and supposedly clean, but that only means clever clean to the examining eye. Al thinks he's still as bent as a broken corkscrew. You can't cross guys like that."

"Yes, I can," Bonnie said, "and I will."

"Did I mention these are probably very bad men, especially Mullen?"

"I don't care if he's Mr. Oedipus T. Rex. I'm taking Little Al and Tanner and am boogying off to Buffalo. Now, are you with me?"

"Of course I am." Maury glanced around the inside of Al's house. He felt comfy and safe there, but he'd learned that could be an illusion. He trusted Bonnie more than his own craving for the creature comfort of staying put. "Should we call Al?"

"No. Chances are these guys are hip enough to tap our line to use that against us, and the burner phones Al got the last time are locked in the gun safe. We'll have to connect with Al and Fergie later, once we're outta here."

"Okay, then." Maury stood and handed Little Al to Bonnie. He started toward the stairway down to their quarters.

"Pack as light as you can."

"Spare underwear it is, and that's it. How about you?"

"Oh, come back here and hold Little Al. I'll pack for us."

Maury had Little Al in his papoose strapped to his own chest when Bonnie came up the stairs carrying one small duffel bag. Her Smith & Wesson Chief's Special was tucked into the front of her belt, and she went into Al's bedroom and started to take Al's Glock from his bedside stand. "Nope. I'd better leave that for him," she said. "Okay, let's go."

"Are we going to take Fergie's car?"

"Of course not. They'd spot that in half a heartbeat. We'll go through the woods like ol' Dan'l Boone." She handed him the small duffel to carry.

"How will we go on from there?"

"Something will occur. You'll see."

"You know what might help? Maybe give Little Al and me a flash of boob before we go."

"You're a boob. Now, c'mon," she said. "Remember, if we get spotted, smile like someone who still has all his own teeth."

"I do have all my own teeth."

"Then use them. Let's go."

Outside the front door, she held Tanner's leash and slipped off into the nearest thick patch of woods, on a path she must have taken before.

Maury stayed as close as he could. Bonnie was letting Tanner sniff away, in case any of the guards they'd spotted earlier had moved. They were careful not to let their steps crunch on the loose leaf litter or break any of the small fallen twigs. Small wildflowers had started to bloom, welcoming the warmer weather of spring, which came in February in their part of America.

Bonnie paused now and then to peer into the woods around them, steering away from spots indicated by Tanner as occupied by those keeping an eye out for intruders coming toward the house. Maury supposed those guys were less geared for people slipping away from the house, at least for the time being.

Fortunately, not all the trees were deciduous. The live oaks and mountain cedars had kept their thick, concealing green, enough to hide them as they kept away from the lane yet eased toward the main road. The woods seemed quieter than usual, held in a preternatural stillness with none of the twitter of birds or scamper of lizards bustling through the dry leaf litter. The wind did rustle the upper limbs of trees and toss loose leaves and the dry sticks of those bushes still in bare-limb winter mode.

Off to their right, a twig snapped and someone coughed. Then Maury heard voices that seemed to be coming closer. At least a couple of people were moving about.

They couldn't veer to their left. Tanner had indicated people in that direction. They could only try to go faster straight ahead.

Bonnie paused and nodded for him to take the lead, probably since he was carrying Little Al. She hung back to protect them from the rear.

He wasn't sure which way to go, but Bonnie stayed close enough to reach out and grab the shoulder of his jacket to steer him.

Ahead, a lump of white became a truck parked in enough thick brush to hide it from the road. It was an older Dodge Ram. He checked the doors.

"Locked," he whispered.

Bonnie was already bent down and feeling along the inside of the back bumper. She shook her head.

Maury moved to the gas cap. The truck was old enough that the flap didn't lock from the inside. He opened it and felt around. *Aha!* He pulled a small metal box loose from its nesting place and held it up to rattle it.

Bonnie grabbed the box, took out the spare key, and opened the driver's side while Maury scurried around to the other side. He climbed in, pushing Tanner and his wagging tail to one side as Bonnie started the truck. She put it in gear, and they shot out of the woods, pausing only long enough for her to look both ways. Then she pulled out onto the road, fastening her seat belt as she did.

Maury glanced back, expecting to see men rushing out onto the road with weapons. But the road was clear.

"Whew," he said. "Someone is going to be plenty riled when they find their truck is gone."

"Into each life some rain must fall. I'm just glad the shower is on them so they can be mad enough to chew nails and spit out a barbed-wire fence instead of doing anything to us."

"Where to now?" Maury asked.

"I think we're off to see the rabbit people. Yeah, that's the ticket." Bonnie glanced toward Little Al. "The rabbit people."

Chapter Eight

A l found a parking spot in one of the municipal garages. The spot was big enough for his truck and, amazingly enough, in the shade of a lower floor, as opposed to being in the sun on the top floor, so they wouldn't have to return to an Easy-Bake Oven of a vehicle. He and Fergie climbed out of the truck, went down two flights of cement stairs, and walked through the city and state buildings to see the district clerk of courts, who kept the records of felonies and some misdemeanors for the county.

"Coming down here to this cluster of government buildings gathered like chicks around the hen of the capital building always makes me think of 'Big Jim' Hogg." Al nodded up at the five-story building they were passing.

"Really? Your memory goes back that far?" she asked.

"Of course not. You know he was governor in the eighteen-nineties."

"I've always heard about his daughter, Ima. That was an awfully cruel thing to name a girl."

"I doubt he thought about it much, or at all. In any case, the rumor that he also had a daughter named Ura is, and always has been, false."

Fergie had heard that Texas urban myth often enough that it didn't even rouse a begrudging chuckle.

They went inside the building, which had that funky, officious smell Al associated with aged structures of its type—years of dust, astringent cleaning products applied by custodians in the night, and the whiff of lingering fear from the many people who'd passed through its halls in their less than happy moments.

At last, they entered an open room where a number of clerks were doing their busywork as registrars, recorders, and custodians of all the paperwork generated by any number of legal actions, ranging from petty to far more serious. When Al asked to see the district clerk of courts in person, he got a raised eyebrow from a matronly woman who might well have spent a lifetime working in the building and rarely heard such a request.

Without having to flash any badges—which he and Fergie both had but were careful enough not to use in such a place since the authority behind them had passed when they'd retired—they were at last led to the office of Bishop Rawley, the district clerk of courts.

"Oh, it's you." Rawley stood from behind his desk but didn't wave them to either of the scarred wooden captain's chairs on the other side of his desk, nor to the once-burgundy leather sofa, which looked like it had been slept on quite a few times.

Rawley was a tall, lanky man who wore bow ties. Al had tried before to decide if he was seeking to emulate Bill Nye, the Science Guy, or Orville Redenbacher, the popcorn guy. His white shirt looked heavily starched, and his suit pants had the severe crease of a recent ironing. He reached for his suit jacket, which hung on a wooden valet behind the desk, and tugged it on. As his hand came through the jacket sleeve, it flashed a big signet ring, a raised cameo with heavy gold mounting, which he wore on his right forefinger. Then he buttoned the middle button.

"To what do I owe this visit?"

Al glanced toward Fergie. She, too, had picked up on Rawley avoiding the word "honor."

The tension between him and Al was palpable. Rawley had gotten a degree in criminal justice years before and tried to become a sheriff's deputy. Al was the one who had to wash him out. Rawley was way overeager and dangerous to be around. He charged through the academy tests and exercises, fired his gun unnecessarily several times, and badgered the other would-be deputies.

He went on to law school and, in time, ran for the district clerk's office. He was a fresh new face at a time when the quicksand of politics was shifting, and he got elected. Maybe the bow tie helped. He'd held the position for twenty-three years.

Without going into Victor's theory about one person being behind the many petty crimes, Al took a folded paper out of his back pocket, a list of those who fit the profile of crimes backed by someone assuring them bail or a lawyer if caught. "I wonder if you or someone on your staff could help check a few individuals who have trickled through the system."

The corner of Rawley's mouth twitched, what Al took for a suppressed smile. "Sure. The usual fee is ten dollars per name searched, going back ten years, with up to three AKAs. Any additional AKAs are ten dollars more, each. You can get one of those in the outside office you just passed through to do that. You didn't need to come to me." He was one of those people who thought speaking in a monotone made him sound more serious.

"I was hoping you could help for free. I'm trying to find some sort of pattern here." He was thinking human trafficking or anyone deported to other countries.

Rawley just stood there like a hesitant piece of Stonehenge, waiting to be understood at some far future date.

"Can you help?" Al tried again.

The mouth corner twitched again. "I can hardly do your job for you, particularly insomuch as it is not even a job but some retiree version of thinking of yourself as some sort of caped crusader."

"Are you sure?" Al asked. "Not even for old time's sake?"

"Not even if they were good old times."

Al couldn't tell if Rawley's thin lips had twisted into a smirk or if he was showing the disdain of having just bitten into a sour quince.

As they left the building, stepping out into the dry air of a day where the temperature had climbed ten or more degrees while they'd been inside, Fergie asked, "You guys aren't exactly chums, are you?"

"You picked up on that, did you?"

Chapter Nine

Bonnie drove the stolen truck, glancing often at Little Al, still in his papoose on Maury's chest. Tanner crowded the floorboards at Maury's feet, trying from time to time to get up on his lap but getting pushed back down. The roads got smaller and narrower with each turn Bonnie took into backwoods parts of Texas Maury had never seen before.

"Just where in blazes do these rabbit people live?" Maury looked around at the roadside around them.

"Out at the very ends of the civilized world, where there's room for hutches and not many people can pop in to bother them. It's why they seemed a natural for folks on the lam, such as ourselves."

Maury hadn't seen as much of the county as Al had in his years in the sheriff's department, and he was pretty certain he'd never, ever been to the locale they seemed headed to, nor had he wanted to head out to those parts. Bonnie turned right, and the two-lane road they'd been on became an even narrower, less-maintained one. Pieces of the asphalt had fallen off into a ditch on one side, looking like bites out of a licorice bar. Weeds and brush grew all the way to the edge of the road, leaving no room for a shoulder.

Then she turned again onto an even smaller road. At the corner, Maury noticed a collapsing sign for Eddie's Bent Eagle Fish Camp—not very promising.

The occasional cottages they passed didn't encourage him either. They looked unoccupied and were all losing a battle to weather, wind, sun, and gravity.

They passed an office that was perhaps occupied, but not by people proud enough to sit on the drooping wooden porch. The road continued to narrow until it became dirt and gravel, mostly dirt. On rainy days, it was almost certainly a real slip-and-slide of a drive.

At last, they seemed to be running out of road, with glimpses of the lake showing through now and again through a smattering of trees, thick brush, and tall grasslands turning into a wetland along the shore.

Ahead, a double-wide trailer looked to be the centerpiece of rows of hutches and a low livestock barn where Maury could see one or two goats, each vying to stand on top of an overturned rusty wheelbarrow.

A white Cadillac was parked right in front of the house, a stark contrast to the worn brown home with lopsided red shutters. A woman stepped out onto the wooden deck that served as a porch when she heard their truck approach.

Bonnie pulled in behind the caddie and parked, turned off the engine, and opened her door. "Sally!" she yelled when she got out her side.

"Well, I'll be dipped in dough and made into a nut," Sally said.

Maury got out his side, holding Tanner's leash in one hand and the small backpack holding their belongings in the other.

Sally's eyes fixed on Maury in a way that seemed to take in everything about him, particularly his age. Her eyes swept back to the much younger Bonnie then to the baby in the papoose on Maury's chest.

Maury glanced toward Bonnie, wondering where she'd come across the rabbit people, who weren't the sort to get out and mingle much, more the sort to dart back inside if a door squeaked.

Sally looked like she might well have been made from dough. She was a tall woman though perhaps not as tall as Fergie. But she was the sort who probably referred to herself as big-boned. Her blond hair was natural and hung down straight on all sides from the part in the middle. She'd added highlights of bright pink, red, and purple to the sides and tips of her hair. Her body sloped down into a soft, wide pear shape, the waist undulating beneath her green T-shirt as she came down the stairs of the deck. Her peasant skirt flared out to emphasize rather than diminish the rest of her. As she got nearer and embraced Bonnie, Maury saw Sally had an upside-down U of a nose ring with two bright-green knobs on each end of it.

Some people strove to be unique, and she'd pulled out all the stops to be at the head of that class.

The male half of the pair stepped out onto the porch and started down the wooden stairs. He was taller than Sally and had long, shaggy dark hair, scruffy clothes, and a long wispy beard that hung down his chest like a wrinkled black tube sock.

He was thin enough to look like he would rattle if he fell, the opposite of Sally's lumpy pale flesh.

As he came up to them, he said, "My name's Buck."

"No, it's not." Sally gave him a push.

"That was just some rabbit humor," the guy said.

"Are you sure?" Maury asked.

"Well, naw. It's Tom." When he turned to hold out a hand to Maury, his nose twitched, just the way a rabbit's would.

These people spend way too much time around rabbits.

Maury caught a whiff of moldy straw and a faint aroma of animals that came either from the rabbits or the goats.

"We need a place to stay and kind of hide out," Bonnie said.

Sally and Tom glanced toward each other, then she turned back to Bonnie. "Well, sure."

Just that short hesitation—but the couple seemed like nice, caring people who just happened to know a good deal about rabbits.

"How many rabbits do you have?" Maury couldn't help asking.

"Forty-three, as of this morning," Sally said, "but you know rabbits. There could be fifty by now."

Maury nearly asked if they sold them for the meat, but a glance from Bonnie stifled that, as if she'd been reading his mind.

"We can put you in our room. Tom's been wanting to set up the tent for us to take a whirl at camping."

"I couldn't dream of kicking you out of your own quarters," Bonnie said.

"Don't think twice about it. We love an adventure and a fire outside as the evening settles in." Sally led the way inside.

Maury didn't know whether to take Tanner along or not, so he held the leash and followed. Tanner hadn't shown any desire to have a go at the rabbits or goats. He was that way with the rabbits, squirrels, and deer around their own place—pretty laissez-faire about the whole thing, live and let live. He just seemed happy to have a home and not be at the rescue center anymore, where he'd been only a couple of days from being euthanized.

As they crossed the deck, Sally glanced back at the truck they'd come in. "Is that truck...?"

"It's as hot as hush puppies right out of the deep fryer," Bonnie said.

"Leave the keys in it. I'll have Tom park it around back."

Tom nodded, twitched his nose, and started to head toward the truck.

"Best see to the tent first," Sally called out to him.

Inside the house, Maury could hear and smell rabbits. Some of the inside doors were closed, but through those ajar he could see cages piled up to the ceilings.

"We keep the kits inside and any of the does or bucks that need special attention," Sally said.

Everything in their house was about rabbits. Posters, ceramic figurines, decorated plates, and photographs were everywhere, as well as stuffed-rabbit toys along the couch pillows. The carpet was green with a pattern of scattered Easter eggs and rabbits.

"Do you know what's missing here?" Maury leaned close to whisper to Bonnie.

"Hard to believe anything is. But what?" she whispered back.

"Rabbit ears for the television."

She jabbed him in the ribs with an elbow, careful to miss Little Al.

In the bedroom, the bed was a king-sized mattress on the floor, with rumpled sheets. Maury wondered if Sally would have bothered to make the bed if she knew she was going to have company. He decided probably not. Theirs was a casual but happy world.

A tiny crib beside the bed contained a small rabbit. Sally picked up the crib. "I'll just take this little fellow to another room. I've been keeping an eye on him." She glanced around, shrugged, and said, "Make yourselves to home."

Maury went over to the window and pulled the blinds to one side. Tom was outside, setting up a tent in front of a wide metal bowl where they probably had fires.

"I feel bad about displacing the rabbit people," Maury said. "To give up their own bedroom like that is really something."

Tanner curled up in one corner and watched them.

Bonnie came over to take Little Al out of his papoose. "Once you get a closer look at this bed, you might have second thoughts about that. Maybe we could talk them out of the tent... if I didn't have a little one to fret about."

With the papoose still hanging off his chest, Maury stepped closer to the bed and looked at it. "Do you think they'd take offense if we ran their sheets and blankets through the washer and dryer before we use them?"

Before she could answer, Tanner gave a low growl. Maury tilted his head then went to the window and pulled aside the blind.

Sally and Tom had abruptly stopped putting up their tent. They stood still, heads snapping left to right in rapid jerks. Together, they moved quietly but quickly toward the thickest copse of woods near them and disappeared into the green.

"Uh oh," Maury said.

Tanner's growl grew louder.

The door to their room started to open.

Tanner sprang to his feet, growling, and took off across the room. Maury grabbed at the dog's leash and caught it in time. Tanner strained at it, planting all four feet, and snarled.

Three large men entered the room. The hair of each was buzz cut as short as an electric razor could get it. Their bodies showed thick muscles from much time in a gym, or prison yard, and their faces showed no emotion, none whatsoever. Their eyes didn't blink. The tattoos Maury could see didn't encourage him. Part of a swastika and a bit of Hitler's face peeped out from the white T-shirt sleeves of the nearest ones. Two of the men held AR-15s, low in their hands, but where they could swing them up before Bonnie could get to her gun.

One seemed to be the leader. "I wouldn't get too settled," he said. "You're coming with us."

"I don't think so," Bonnie said.

The leader turned to her. "I do." A scar ran down in a slash across his face, from the left side of his forehead down to his chin. He must have closed his eyes when he'd been cut, or he would've been wearing an eye patch. Even without it, he looked as mean as a bucket of scorpions.

She glanced down at Little Al in her arms then looked back up. "Okay, then."

She carried the baby over and put him back in the papoose on Maury's chest.

One of the men stepped closer to her and took the gun from inside her belt. He nodded toward the backpack. Another guy poked around inside the pack and found mostly diapers and formula. He dropped the pack back onto the bed then took their cell phones and set them on silent, but didn't crush them as Maury expected. Instead, he left them on and slid them under the bed.

Tanner pulled harder at the leash.

"Shh. Shh," Maury said.

"If that dog succeeds in biting me, he's gonna be the deadest dog that ever looked cross-eyed at a pork chop." The leader turned and started back out the door.

Bonnie picked up their backpack and followed. "Where are Sally and Tom now?"

Maury shook his head. "Rabbit people are no good in a showdown with thugs like these guys."

As they stepped out onto the deck and started down the steps, Maury asked, "How did you find us?"

The leader paused to frown at him. "All our vehicles have GPS trackers now."

That was the last anyone spoke as they were loaded into a white windowless van, while one of the Aryans went over to recover their pickup truck. The van's engine started, and they were off. Maury sat facing the back, as did Bonnie, with Tanner between them. They couldn't tell where they were headed, nor did they have any idea what might happen next.

The man sitting with them in the back of the van had a swastika tattoo on his neck and a gun across his knees and stared at them, saying nothing. He had the kind of nose that had been broken so many times that he might have come to enjoy it. His eyes had narrowed into squinted concentration. Maury couldn't guess whether being in prison or in a war had led to that level of dedication to a task. He certainly didn't feel up to asking.

Tanner kept up a steady low growl the whole time. Bonnie slid her hand down the leash to hold him by the collar so he couldn't lunge at the man guarding them.

Bonnie reached out across Tanner with her other hand and held Maury's.

Chapter Ten

Fergie glanced toward Al as they neared his house, and he slowed his truck. His hands tightened on the steering wheel as he looked carefully into the woods. Fergie looked out her window and did the same.

Al pulled over and took the Sig Sauer out of the glove box. "I'll have a look around. Meet you at the end of the lane."

Fergie slid over to the driver's side, put the truck in gear, and started slowly up the road again. She glanced in the mirror and saw Al disappear into the woods behind her.

In all the years she'd been a detective on the city's police department, with Al in the same role for the county sheriff's department, they'd never worked together on a case. But in recent years, they'd experienced their share of figuring out tangled messes. Her approach was quite different from his. She was prone to develop a hypothesis and then challenge it, proving it right or wrong. With the current situation, she didn't have the beginning of an idea of where to start. The petty criminals were being manipulated and used like a herd of cattle, their crimes making little money, but the volume was adding up to major money being accumulated somewhere. Add to that Kemper Giles being affected enough to risk trying to use Al to find whoever was behind the scenes. Then, sprinkled on top like some sort of toxic whipped cream, the Aryan Brotherhood had added itself to the mix. No way in purple pickled hell did any of it make sense, no matter how she tried to tie any of it together with normal cause and effect.

She kept the truck creeping along slowly. Where the bushes were still green or undergrowth thick enough to hide a vehicle, she slowed even more to peer inside the foliage. A car came up behind her, so she pulled over onto the shoulder then slipped back onto the road once it was past.

One bit of color she spotted turned out to be a scrap of cloth caught on the thorn of a mesquite tree. But she saw no people, vehicles, or any sign of Al.

She turned Al's truck around at the entrance to a lane a mile up the road then headed back to Al's drive. As she turned onto it, Al stepped out from behind a thick cluster of mountain cedar, shaking his head.

He slid into the passenger seat instead of coming around to drive. "Awfully quiet," he said. "Too quiet. Let's go to the house."

The moment they unlocked and stepped inside the front door, Fergie knew something was wrong. Tanner would have, should have been rushing toward them.

She went downstairs while he checked every room on the upper floor. The baby's crib was empty, and the papoose Maury or Bonnie often carried him in was gone. She checked the laundry room—empty as well. Fergie hurried back upstairs.

Al stood in the middle of the living room, looking around and holding his Glock in his left hand. "Something must have made them head for the hills. But they didn't take your car."

"They could have just gotten antsy."

"I tried to call. Their phones aren't taking calls."

"But they're on?"

"Yeah."

"Then we can find them."

"I'm just wondering," he said.

"What?"

"If that isn't just what's expected of us."

KEEPING AN EYE ON THE GPS, Fergie told Al to take the next right.

"I don't like where this is headed," he said. "Have you ever been out this way before?" Fergie looked up. Nothing looked the least bit familiar, and the farther out on the back roads they went, the more turned around and lost she felt.

"Oh, I suppose I've been to every nook and cranny of this county at one time or another. Those two burned-out places we passed a ways back were meth labs once."

"Any crack houses out here?"

"Nope. Too far to drive. But they make the stuff out here when they can. The deputies on patrol usually sent up a flag, and the rest of us would swoop in."

"You think Bonnie, Maury, Little Al, and Tanner are in a place like that?"

"I'm hoping not. There's one other place they might be, and it's as way the hell out here as you can get."

"What are you thinking of?"

The road narrowed until it tapered away and disappeared beside one last residence. A fairly new white Cadillac sat parked in front of a weathered brown double-wide trailer with fading red shutters. Rows of hutches and a low livestock barn crowded close behind.

"The rabbit people," Al said. "Why did they turn to the rabbit people? And how did they get here?"

"The GPS blip says they're still here," Fergie said. "And who are the rabbit people?"

"When our animal-control people had special issues, they sometimes called on specialists for cattle, goats, and many other forms of wildlife. These are the people they called upon when they had rabbit issues, Sally and Tom Crawfordson. And here they come."

Two people came out from behind the house, from the direction of a lake visible through the woods and cattails along its edge.

Al opened his door and got out where they could see him.

"Whew." Sally wiped a hand across her forehead. "I thought that was you. I seen you through the winder and just hoped those others hadn't come back."

"What others?" Al asked.

Fergie got out and went to stand beside Al while glancing at her phone. The fellow was about as tall as she was though his shoulders were stooped as if that rag of a beard was pulling him toward the ground. Fergie blinked at the woman's kaleidoscope of hair color and her stout, soft, downward-sloping build. Her eyes fixed on the two bright-green dots of Sally's nose ring and stayed fixed there no matter how hard she tried to look away.

"Them Nazis," Tom said.

Sally gave him a look, and his mouth clamped shut behind the beard.

"Where's Bonnie and the others, Sally?" Al stared toward the house.

"They took 'em away. What could we do?" Sally frowned while Tom quivered in place, his nose twitching.

They're rabbits themselves, Fergie thought but kept it to herself. She could smell goats, too, but the wet straw and rabbit smell prevailed. She blamed it on the wind. "Do you mind if we take a look?" she asked.

"Knock yourselves out," Sally said. "I'm a-telling you they done been yanked out of the hat."

Al and Fergie stepped around them and went up onto the deck porch and right into the house. As was the way of rabbit people, they trailed closely behind.

In the bedroom, Fergie crouched low on the floor, reached under the bed, and pulled out two cell phones. She turned them off. "They were left here for a reason," she said.

Al nodded and turned to Sally. "Any idea where they were taken?"

She shook her head.

"You said Nazis." Al looked at Tom. "Why?"

"You know, the usual tattoos in bad taste, just the sort of thing to declare a hate-driven side when in prison."

"Where were you when you saw the men who came?"

Tom lowered his head. "In the woods."

"Probably just as well," Al said. "You couldn't have stopped these men and might've gotten hurt. And you have no idea where they took them?"

Sally and Tom shook their heads in unison, causing the green dots of the nose ring to sway on Sally. Fergie looked away.

As they climbed back into Al's truck, Fergie asked, "Now what?"

He shook his head and shrugged. But he started the truck, turned it around, and started down the lane. They had to go somewhere. Fergie had no idea where. She'd dealt with the Aryan Brotherhood a few times in her city-cop days. They always seemed on the move. That probably hadn't changed much, given how they went about spreading joy and love wherever they went.

Chapter Eleven

The great manipulator. The master puppeteer. He could only imagine the names they were calling him as he strolled past a park on
his way from his office to his house and his den within, where he made
it all happen and was quietly becoming one of the richest and most
powerful people he could have ever imagined.

On the far side of the park, a group of children squealed and ran
after each other. He ignored them.

A woman pushing a baby carriage passed on the sidewalk, going the
other way. Instead of peeking inside for anything like a warm and fuzzy
feeling, he had to fight back a sneer. A nonsmoker and nondrinker, he'd
not had anything like relations with women since an ill-fated episode in
college with a Jezebel he'd caught in the lewd and physical act of cheat-
ing on him. Both had been naked and squirming around like earth-
worms in the rain. Even at the thought, his hands started to curl into
fists, but that wasn't how he fought his fights.

That lesson had been harsh and graphic enough to prevent him
from trusting women ever again, but not drastic enough to cause him
to seek comfort among men. He currently possessed a gender-free ha-
tred of his fellow humans, which included the confused ones who
didn't know which way they truly leaned. He had a new love and joy in
his life, and it was money, and it was power. Of course, it included using others as an extra little treat.

Sometimes he felt like a giant spider at the center of a web, a web of
his own making. He took a deep, exhilarating breath. Life was good...
for him.

As he got to the end of his walk, he looked up and down the street in front of his house. *Nothing. Good.*

He went inside and locked the front door, which looked like wood but wasn't—not that he expected battering rams at any moment. The steel just made him more comfortable and happier—if happiness was a real thing for him. Gloating pride was more like it, which swelled as he went right to the room that mattered most, his den.

He took out a key and unlocked the door. He could tell he'd upset others in the world, ones who would like to see harm come to him. He would've laughed out loud at them if he was prone to laughter, which he wasn't.

Along one wall sat a line of computers, but they would never get to him that way. While he hadn't started out as an IT expert, he'd studied and learned every firewall and technique that could bounce his signals through a maze of satellites and around the world several times.

Aside from that and the boxes and boxes of burner phones on the shelves across the room, he considered himself an old-fashioned sort of guy.

From the masses of data he'd sorted through, his desk held three color-coded Rolodexes. Within minutes of a new need or a fresh idea, he could reach out to an eager bail bondsman or attorney or recidivist ex-con, who would respond with whatever he wanted, depending on the expertise and past experiences of his many minions, whom he could move around on a chessboard only he understood.

The combination of the newest technology and his old-school methods contributed to a screen that meant no one could touch him, ever. No Cayman Island accounts or shell companies for him, either. He kept everything there in that room, where he could get to it and also savor how very, very rich he had become.

A four-hundred-pound black antique safe advertising the American Safe and Lock Co. in red, yellow, and gold letters stood almost a yard high, dominating one corner of the room, its combination-locked hundred-pound door closed at the moment. He'd bought it at an estate sale for a doctor and had paid way too much. But it was exactly the kind of thing he'd pictured in his head. His money was never farther away than that.

Using cash and untraceable money orders was important to his pickups and providing bail or lawyer money. His system didn't always work. Some people bucked or were stingy. Those who failed to play fair on their end found themselves with no bail or support. Any who tried to double-cross him and catch him only met another of his minions. It was a numbers game, after all, but one that eventually skewed to his favor. Sure, he dealt with losers, flakes, and cons, but most came through, and they could often be used again. Even if by some stretch they might figure out who he was, which they couldn't, they would no doubt consider him a benign overlord, an ally, a far opposite of those in law enforcement.

He'd built up a core of reliable petty criminals with specific skills, sufficiently short rap sheets, and the right amount of greed combined with fear of getting caught. The Rolodex nearest him attested to that, with its color-coded tabs sorted by talent and proclivity. He used multiple layers of couriers and runners instead of any methods that might be traced. He was always seven steps or more away, safe and invulnerable.

Setting up an escape plan had never been necessary. Even with a few recent flutters, he was far from ever being discovered. He figured he might put something together someday, but for the moment, he savored fending off the futile efforts of any who tried, while every day he became richer and more powerful than they could ever imagine being in their sad little lives.

Years before, he'd caught himself rubbing his hands together briskly whenever he reveled at the secret life he lived. He made himself stop doing it, especially in public, where a satisfied, even eager expression might accompany the rubbing. But he indulged himself for just a moment and rubbed his palms together until they were warm. Then he sat down at his desk to do more of God's work, he himself being the god.

Chapter Twelve

The motel-room door closed behind them with a harsh metallic click. Maury had seen one of the two Aryan guards in the hallway glancing back inside as the door closed and Tanner had given them one final low growl.

Maury went over to the door with Little Al still in the papoose on his chest. The baby's Binky had fallen out and he started to cry without it. Maury put the pacifier in range of the little mouth, which sucked it back into place.

Little Al closed his eyes and made contented *mm, mm, mm* sounds.

Maury felt the edges of the door. *Steel on steel.* That sure wasn't a good sign. He turned to see Bonnie coming out of the tiny bathroom on the other side of the two twin beds. Tanner was sniffing at every surface though the room didn't have that many.

"I sure don't trust these guys," Bonnie said.

Maury looked around the room. "In a world where it's gotten far too easy to hate, these guys epitomize the angriest form of it. Maybe in prison they had to band together out of fear, to protect themselves against other tight groups. But they've taken their arrogant ignorance further back to when Hitler pumped up the notion of a superior and exclusive race, with all others as enemies to be eliminated. So trust them? I think not."

As Maury took inventory, he saw no television or radio and certainly no telephone. The walls were bare. He went to the one window. *Yep.* It had the crisscross of wrought-iron bars screwed into place from outside. The place looked like a room in a cheap motel, but it was solid and simple and felt more like a prison cell.

A wooden dresser and desk had been built along one wall, but no chair sat there.

"Not even a pad and pencil," Maury said, "or you could be rewriting *The Diary of Anne Frank*."

Bonnie didn't say anything. Her lower lip began to quiver.

"Oh my gosh. I forgot your telling me how your grandparents slipped out of Poland just before..."

He went over to her and turned sideways to put his arms around her without crushing Little Al.

Tanner came closer and looked up at them, letting out a low, sympathetic whine.

One of Bonnie's arms moved down to stroke the dog's fur.

They stood like that for a while, neither able to say a word.

She finally took half a step back and reached to take Little Al out of the papoose. Holding him, she eased down to sit on one of the beds.

Al went to look out the window again. Tanner followed, pressing his side against Maury's leg. The view offered little hope. The copse of old woods pressing right up to what was clearly a former motel looked bleak and dark, overgrown with weeds, thorny bushes, and limbs broken and collapsed in on each other.

Maury felt at the edges of the window then went back to the door and twisted the knob. It was locked and didn't open. He sighed and turned to Bonnie. She was patting Little Al and cooing to him, but a single tear ran down one cheek.

He went and sat beside her. Tanner moved close and pressed his snout in where their thighs touched, trying to get as close to them as he could.

They sat like that for a long time, far too long.

Maury finally said, "Al's always talking about something way out there, like those Japanese Noh plays where time stretches out in slow motion like taffy. I never understood entirely what he meant before."

Neither had a cell phone, and Bonnie hadn't worn her watch. But Maury still wore his trusty Timex, which kept on ticking. He found himself glancing at it far too often. Nothing happened, though, until almost five in the afternoon.

A low growl started in Tanner's throat. Maury reached down and took hold of the leash. After a click, the door unlocked. One of the thick Aryan guards swung the door open, while another just as big stood behind him. Tanner's growl grew louder, but Maury held the leash tightly.

A small blond girl came into the room carrying a tray, which she placed on the desk. When she turned, she pointed at Tanner. Maury frowned then caught on. Tanner wasn't growling at her.

Up close, her blond hair was wispy thin. She wore thick, black-rimmed glasses and had a harelip, the flesh puckered like a scar just above her mouth. Though she had the very pale skin of a blonde, something about her face was foreign, which Maury couldn't place. She pointed again and made walking motions with her fingers but never said a word.

He figured out what she meant and handed her the leash. Tanner would need to get outside now and then for his bathroom breaks. She walked him out the door, keeping a firm grip on the leash so that he couldn't get at the men.

The door closed behind her with its click of finality, which was starting to become familiar.

Bonnie carried Little Al across the room and lifted the plastic cover from the tray. "Oh my."

Maury moved closer to look. A thin green plastic bowl held dry dog food. Beside it were two plastic-wrapped sandwiches of bologna and wilting lettuce, from a vending machine. A couple of plastic bottles of water and two small packages of saltine crackers rounded out the smorgasbord before them.

"I hardly know where to start," Bonnie said.

"Maybe with Tanner's dry food." Maury gave one of the wrapped sandwiches a push with a finger.

But hunger won out, and they managed to finish off the sandwiches, the crackers, and most of the water by the time the door cracked open and Tanner came surging in.

The girl followed and went to pick up the tray. As she turned, Bonnie handed Little Al to Maury and stepped closer to the girl. Her hands went into a flurry of motions.

The girl's eyes opened wider, and she shared her first smile. She put the tray down, and her own hands got busy in a whir that matched Bonnie's.

Maury watched, fascinated.

Then the door opened, and the guard leaned in.

The girl snatched up the tray, whirled, and shot out of the room. The door clicked shut behind her.

"What were you doing?" Maury asked.

"Turns out she knows American Sign Language even though she's not American."

"What did you say?"

"I said, 'Thank you.' Then she told me a bit about herself. She's from the Philippines."

"And that's it?"

"She said she is Patty Belle."

"That's her name?"

"It's the one they gave her."

"What do these guys want?" Maury asked. "Why whisk us away and hold onto us?"

"I think you know the answer."

"Yeah. We're some kind of bargaining chip. I guess they'll be nice to us for a while... until they don't need us any longer."

Bonnie started to say something but wasn't able to speak. She held Little Al more tightly, and they sat in silence for a while with Tanner pressing closer, seeming aware of how they felt.

Finally breaking the silence, Maury said, "Al says these guys formed up as an alliance in prisons. They're a hate group to do battle against the other hate groups, the gangs, the blacks, the Latinos, and just about anyone not in their little neo-Nazi circle."

"So they're not the good guys. I get that."

"No. They are far, far from being the good guys."

"Are they honorable, though? Do you think they'll just let us go if they manage to make Al and Fergie do what they want?"

"Well, Al never mentioned if they were honorable or not. But he did tell me some truly nasty things that happened in prison. So if I had to bet on it, I'd say no. These guys are neither good nor honorable."

As soon as the sky grew dark outside their window, they climbed into the two beds. Although Bonnie had Little Al with her, Tanner chose to ease up onto the end of that bed and curl up at her feet.

Maury lay there with his eyes wide open for the longest time. Nothing he could think of helped him relax enough to drop off to sleep. He tried ocean waves, then the color green, followed by the color blue. *Nothing.*

He thought about their chances of getting out of where they were. He even wondered about what was in it for the Aryans and why they might keep their word if everyone did what they wanted. That was no way to get to sleep, so he stopped. Then he wondered for a stretch about Al and Fergie—where they were and what they were doing and what they'd thought when they found Bonnie and he weren't still at the house.

Maury's eyes snapped open in the night. He thought he'd heard something, a scream. While still trying to establish what had made the noise, he heard three loud thumps, like someone getting beaten.

Enough light was coming in through the window for him to see even though it was still nighttime.

He turned to see Bonnie's eyes open wide. She held Little Al asleep in her arms. "We've got to get out of here."

Maury couldn't disagree.

Chapter Thirteen

After Al dialed, the phone rang five times before Victor finally picked up.

"You again?" Victor let out a huff of air.

"I need some help here." Al glanced toward Fergie, who was sitting patiently in the truck's passenger seat, seeming amused by him asking for help.

"That's what we're here for. Your local charitable sheriff's department."

"Some people's lives may depend upon it. Do you know anything about where the Aryan Brotherhood might be at the moment? They move around a lot."

"This really important?"

"Of course it is," Al snapped.

"Okay. Okay. Well, I can't tell you."

Al sighed.

"But if I were you," Victor said, "I'd stay away from the old Bryson spread out at the west edge of the county."

"Gotcha."

Fergie looked at him when he hung up. "What have you got?"

"Another one of those dark corners."

She raised an eyebrow.

"It's what used to be called the Bryson spread, with one end almost hanging off the edge of the county. Old Buford Bryson was in the Texas Nationalist Movement and also had ties to the Aryan Brotherhood. He wanted an all-white Texas to leave the United States. We weren't called out to his place all that much because he kept to himself. He had his

own gun range, and the ATF kept half an eye on him, but as he got older, he was mostly bluster and hot air. Then he passed away a few years
ago, and I haven't heard much about the place since."

"Did Victor tell you to go there?"

"No. He said to stay away."

"Well, that was sure a piece of red wool dangled in front of a cat."

Al started the truck and pulled out onto the road. "We might as
well go have a look-see."

"How far is it?"

"It's to hell and gone from where we are. The county's a little over a
thousand square miles. I've always heard that most Texas counties were
first measured by the distance a man could ride on horseback from the
county seat to one side or the other in a day. The horsepower of this
truck is over four hundred horses, so it should get us there in less than
an hour even if we have to knock someone off the road and out of the
way."

"Just don't drive like a tomfool."

Al made good time getting across the county without having to
pass anyone or in any other way act the tomfool.

The houses grew fewer and fewer and farther apart, most set way
back from the small road. Where the thick growth played out and
turned into pastureland, the slopes of hills showed waves of bluebonnets and the salmon pink of Indian paintbrush wildflowers running all
the way down to the edges of the road on both sides.

"Hard to believe we're getting farther out into the rough-and-tum-
ble of the county when it just gets prettier," she said.

"We're a couple of weeks ahead of Easter. Soon, families will be driving out to take their annual photos in the bluebonnets."

"I doubt they'll be driving way the hell out here," Fergie said.

"The flowers aren't bothered much out this way—not much building or development going on."

"Oh my gosh. You're thinking about moving out this way, aren't you?"

"We'll see about that when we get where we're going."

A ways before they neared Blanco County, he turned onto a two-lane road with almost no shoulder.

Al had his window open and slowed when he heard gunshots ahead. He glanced at Fergie.

"Too early for the Fourth of July, isn't it?" Her head tilted.

"Those are AR-15s," Al said. "So I'm guessing it isn't a rabbit shoot."

Before they got any closer, Al pulled off onto a lane that headed toward a burned-out barn.

"How did you know about this approach?" Fergie turned to look at him.

"I've probably been in every nasty nook in the county at least once."

"Way out here?"

"More often than I care to mention."

Al snugged the truck up close enough to the far side of the barn, where it couldn't be easily seen, but left room to open their doors. They closed them again with quiet snicks.

He'd taken his Sig Sauer out of the glove box, and he slipped it behind his back. Fergie reached down for a pistol in an ankle holster that wasn't there. She frowned then shrugged.

They started off slowly, bent forward to keep behind what scrub bush existed. The closer they got, the louder the shots sounded. Fergie tilted her head, listening.

Al nodded. "That's right. You're hearing a few different weapons mixed in now. I hear an AK-47 or two and at least one MAC-10. They've got a smorgasbord of various weapons, and they are sure having jolly fun."

"What are they shooting at?"

"Targets."

"Why?"

"Training."

"For what?"

"The war. The big war."

"Against whom?"

"Everyone."

Fergie stopped her slow crouch forward and stood enough to raise an eyebrow.

"You've got to remember"—Al kept his voice low and leaned in closer—"these guys formed up out of fear. It was their hard-headed, buzz-cut selves against every other gang and ethnic group in prison. They get out, and it's just a bigger playing field. It's them against the world. They project hate and get it back, and that makes them paranoid—fierce, angry, and biting-mean paranoid."

After just a few more steps, they could peer through the gaps in a couple of mesquite trees whose chartreuse spring leaves hadn't yet fully crowded in. They did provide some concealment, though, while letting Al and Fergie view a rifle range in the distance with men shooting away.

Al crouched, then Fergie did as well, moving her head close to his.

"There's no law against people discharging firearms on their own land," he said. "We need to see if they're doing anything with the structures out here. That's where Maury, Bonnie, Tanner, and Little Al would be if they were brought out this way."

"Where are the buildings?"

"Over to our left, a couple hundred yards through that thickest patch of mountain cedar and scrub growth. We couldn't just drive in that way."

"Why do I suspect you've taken this particular back way before?"

He eased them to their left as they moved forward, getting farther from where the men were shooting. But he listened closely for the crunch of leaves or the snap of a twig. Some of those Aryans could as easily be doing drills through the woods.

Every nerve felt stretched as tight as piano wire. He glanced toward Fergie. She felt it too. The skin of her face was tight across her cheekbones, her eyes were open wider, and she kept turning her head to listen first in one direction then another.

Near the buildings, Al slowed and pulled aside a drooping coniferous limb, getting the juniper smell of it on his hand and arm. Where the house and other structures had been, he could see only black scorched earth. Everything that had been there was gone.

What had been Old Buford Bryson's legacy was just so much ashy soil.

Fergie pressed close to look over his shoulder.

"What do you suppose happened to the place?"

"I don't know," he whispered back. "But none of those we're looking for can be kept there."

As soon as he stopped speaking, he heard a quiet stillness descend on the woods. He could hear the wind moving the treetops in a rhythm, but all the bird sounds, even the rustle of the occasional lizard, was gone. It had gotten quiet—too quiet.

The last time he'd experienced such a shift in the sounds of the woods, he'd been seconds from being ambushed.

Al heard a rustle and spun, almost knocking Fergie down, but she caught herself by hanging onto his shoulder.

There, standing just a few feet away, with his finger to his lips, stood Victor Kahlon. He waved a hand for them to follow.

They moved as stealthily as before.

For a while, they made good time, even crouched over, then Victor slowed. Al bumped into his back and Fergie into Al. Victor held out the flat of a hand.

Al could hear voices approaching. Soon, he could see two big bruisers, both with shaved heads, wearing matching black T-shirts that had twin lightning bolts in the middle framed by the words Support Your

Local... Repeat Offender. They both carried long weapons, probably ARs.

Al and Fergie dropped as quietly and quickly as they could to tuck themselves into the shade of loose needles under a mountain cedar, with Victor crouched pressing against them, his hand on the gun at his belt.

The Aryan men were so intent on their comparison of the Houston Texans and the Dallas Cowboys that they walked right by, within five feet of the huddled trio.

As soon as the men had passed and crunched out of sight, Victor rose, brushing at some leaf litter on his slacks. He waved a hand again, and they followed.

As they emerged at last from the woods near the burned-out barn where Al had parked, he saw they had company. Three sheriff's department cruisers sat next to the black Mercedes parked behind Al's truck. Half a dozen deputies were loading flak jackets and other gear back into their trunks.

"We had a SWAT team on standby," Victor said in a low voice, "but it turned out we didn't need them."

Cavander Haley still wore a dark-blue Armani jacket. He was brushing at his sleeves although Al couldn't see any leaves still sticking to him. It was one helluva way to dress for dashing through the springtime woods.

"Well, this has been an utter waste of my time." Cav glared at Al. "What are you doing here?"

Al glanced toward Fergie. He nearly said that friends of theirs had been whisked away by members of the Brotherhood. But that might have led to Cav calling in the feds, who would rush in without caring very much about collateral damage.

Fergie stared at him, waiting.

"What about you? Why are you out here?" Al asked.

"A bit of misinformation," Cav said. "It happens. I thought I encouraged you to stay out of my business."

Fergie nodded to herself, aware now of why Al hadn't asked for help from the career-minded Cav in his suit and tie.

"It was something of a waste of our department's resources as well," Victor said. "If asked, we could have mentioned every structure on the place burned down weeks ago. If they're up to any organized-crime activities, it isn't out here. You could probably make a case out of the fact that, for most of these jaspers, carrying a gun around is a parole violation. But that's not exactly up your alley, is it?"

Cav gave him a sharp glance then shrugged. He went over to his vehicle, got in, and was soon heading out the drive while the deputies got back into their cars.

"Care to share anything, Al?" Victor asked.

"These Aryan Brotherhood guys have Maury, Bonnie, the kid, and even my dog."

"I'll let Clayton know. But you should know, Al, these guys move about. They've been caught out before and have gotten clever. Even I don't know where they're operating at the moment, and as soon as I do, they'll probably scoot for another location. They're still arrogant but have gotten slippery as eels."

"Well, slippery or not, I've got to find them."

"And we may have very little time," Fergie said, to which Al nodded.

Chapter Fourteen

The metal door exaggerated the scratching of a key going into its keyhole and twisting and the lock being opened. Maury sat up straighter and reached for Tanner's leash.

When the door swung open, Patty Belle stood there, holding another tray. A couple of the usual Aryan guards stood behind her, trying to look menacing and not having to try very hard. One was putting a key ring back on his belt.

The girl beamed at Bonnie and started signing with her hands as soon as she put the tray down.

Bonnie ignored the tray, which held a couple of pimiento-cheese sandwiches in their vending-machine wrappers, a couple of bottles of water, and a bowl of food for Tanner, whom Maury was holding back. The dog was growling at the guards but not at the small blond girl moving her hands as fast as she could.

"Slow down," Bonnie muttered and replied with her hands.

While they talked, Maury held Little Al, who was suddenly in a squirmy mood, as well as keeping one hand on Tanner's taut leash as he tugged toward the door.

He watched the young girl's face. Even without the harelip, she might not have been what anyone would call pretty. But she was someone's daughter and perhaps sister. He wondered if she was the product of a US serviceman, with that blond hair and pale skin.

Yet she was pretty after all, in her own way. Behind the black-rimmed glasses, her eyes sparkled with eagerness and delight as Bonnie signed to her, and she also lit up whenever she glanced at Little Al or Tanner. The dog had accepted her at once. The two thugs at the door, who'd been talking, turned to notice Patty Belle's hands rapidly exchanging information with Bonnie.

"Hey, cut that out!" one of the guards yelled.

Patty Belle gave another quick flurry with her hands before she spun and hurried out the door, which the guards clanged shut behind her.

"She seemed to have a lot on her mind." Maury picked up one of the sandwiches and peered endwise into its orange-and-red-flecked filling. "Starved for a chat with someone who could speak her hand-jazz language?"

"I asked her if the guards always stood outside our door. She said no, that they had to roam the hallways and make sure all was going well with the ladies in the rooms and their gentlemen visitors."

"Oh. So this is a motel like that."

"Exactly like that. I suspect they're like her, too, imports. She was told she could come to America like an indentured servant and work as a waitress in a restaurant. But at least she isn't turning tricks, she said, the one benefit of her not being pretty."

"None of that makes me feel better about our being in the hands of this sort of men," Maury said.

"She told me the guards eat their supper just before the gentlemen begin to arrive. That's every evening at five p.m., the only time the hallways are clear."

"That was kind of her to share that." Maury felt the beginning of a grin just starting to twitch into place on his face.

When Patty Belle came in an hour later to pick up their tray, Maury moved back while holding Tanner's leash. Bonnie was bent over, changing Little Al.

Patty Belle tried to sign to her.

"Hey. Hey!" One of the guards snapped and charged toward her.

Tanner growled and surged toward the guard, pulling the leash out of Maury's hand.

The guard swung a foot back, ready to kick Tanner with his large black boot.

The girl stepped in front of the foot and grabbed Tanner's leash before he could get in range of the kick. She bent to pat Tanner on the head before she handed Maury the leash. Then she turned to head out the door with the tray. The guard, who had missed his chance at kicking the dog, swung the back of a hand at her. She expertly ducked, eluding the blow with the practice of someone used to avoiding abuse.

The guard, having missed his chance to kick a dog or hit a little girl, glared at Maury and Bonnie in turn before heading out the door.

As the door closed, Maury stepped toward it and held out a folded bit of cardboard he'd kept back from their sandwich wrappings. The door snicked shut with the white cardboard tab sticking out on their side.

"What did you just do?" Bonnie whispered.

"Bought us a ticket out of here if we get lucky."

The rest of the day seemed to move as slowly as possible. The baby and Tanner both acted restless and twitchy.

At five o'clock, Maury had an eye on his watch. "Okay. Let's go."

They'd packed what little they had. Carrying Little Al on his chest in the carrier, Maury made sure the pacifier was in the baby's mouth to keep him quiet. They'd tied a makeshift muzzle around Tanner's mouth so that he wouldn't bark. Bonnie held the leash and had their backpack over her shoulder.

Maury twisted the door's knob, opened it slowly, and leaned out to look up and down the hallway. *Nothing.*

He waved a hand, and Bonnie followed closely as they went down a short hallway past a defunct soda machine. They headed toward a side exit door. Maury shoved on the door's push bar, and it opened. No alarm sounded. He'd figured as much. The customers needed to have a way out in case of a fire, although the women, many who might well be as young as Patty Belle, would be trapped in their rooms.

The gravel parking lot seemed a mile long, but they veered to their left, away from the motel's front door and any possible security there.

Maury expected someone to spot them at any second and call out. The gravel crunched loudly with each step. After what seemed a slow-motion hour, they finally slipped into the darker shadows of the woods. Maury took several slow, deep breaths. Bonnie was panting as if she'd run a mile.

They angled toward the road but didn't go all the way back. Maury stopped when he caught sight of it and moved them back again until it was out of sight.

"We'll wait here until dark. They haven't any reason to check our room until morning. We should have time to get quite a ways from here."

Bonnie took Little Al out of the papoose and held him. She lowered herself to the base of a large old pecan tree and was futzing around in the backpack after some of his formula.

Maury held up a hand. "Shh."

Still standing, he was keeping a wary eye on the woods behind them and had heard a sound. A twig snapped. Dry leaves crackled under a step. Bonnie's eyes opened wider, but she managed to get the bottle into Little Al's mouth.

Maury looked around for a stick. He saw a big one, but it looked rotten, easily breakable and not the thing to bop on someone's head.

He took a quiet step and was bent toward the ground, looking for a better weapon, when a small figure burst from a nearby clutter of green growth. Tanner didn't growl or surge at his leash. Instead, he wagged his tail.

Patty Belle stood there, leaves dropping from her and with a small tear at the shoulder of her T-shirt. As soon as she was near, she began to sign.

Bonnie nodded and looked at Maury. "She wants to come with us."

Maury sighed. "Well, sure. We can hardly leave her back there with those..."

Bonnie had to let go of the bottle to sign back to Patty Belle, but when she did, the girl's eager grin made her the prettiest little girl Maury had ever seen.

She hustled over to pat Tanner and help Bonnie with the baby. She reached for the bottle and lifted it to the baby's mouth. Just like that, they had a babysitter and all-around assistant.

"Now, all we have to do is get as far away from here as possible, as quickly as we can," Maury said.

They waited until darkness had fairly settled in before creeping out close to the road. Only a few vehicles passed one way or the other. Maury supposed the ones coming toward the motel were customers for whatever kind of business was being run there—human trafficking and enforced prostitution, he figured. That would be something to report when they got away... if they got away.

They walked and walked. When no traffic was passing, they got out onto the road and walked, only to dart back into cover when headlights showed from either direction.

Maury got good at constantly looking ahead and having a hiding place in mind as they walked along, and he didn't think any of the road traffic spotted them.

The going felt slow, but Maury estimated they'd put three to four miles behind them when one more vehicle's sweeping lights came over a hill toward them.

They all scurried toward a stand of sumac and a thick clump of willowlike roadside plants called poverty weed. As the vehicle came up to where they hid, it stopped.

The driver's window of the black Cadillac XTS limousine rolled down, and the driver called toward where they were hiding, "Come on. Get in. We'll get you all away from here. We're friends of Al Quinn."

Maury glanced at Bonnie.

"We're already found," she said. "I say we trust them. We can't be worse off than we were with those Aryans."

They hurried across the shoulder and onto the road, and all of them climbed into the back, Tanner as well. Headlights were coming from the other direction as the limo took off with a soft chirp of tire rubber.

A huge man in the front passenger seat turned around to look at them, his round, squinting face like an upset bowling ball. "Cabe here is your driver. I'm Dom Strobinsky. At your service. We was trying to figure a way of getting you all clear of there, but you gave us quite a boost in that regard."

After a few miles, Maury leaned forward and said, "We don't seem to be heading back in the direction where we live."

"Not to worry. We got a place that's a whole lot safer for you. Right, Cabe?"

Maury couldn't be sure, but the driver seemed to be silently chuckling to himself.

Chapter Fifteen

Fergie glanced over at Al. His fingers were nearly white where they clutched the steering wheel, and his jaw flexed as it tightened, relaxed, and tightened again.

She wanted to say she understood. After reuniting with a brother he hadn't spoken to in twenty years, Al didn't want to lose him, Bonnie, or their baby and—perhaps even more so, irrationally enough—Tanner, the dog he'd rescued a day or so before he was to be euthanized. But words seemed insufficient, so she said nothing.

He finally spoke a few miles later. "This must be something of an immense bummer to you. You go all these years, and when you finally get a marriage proposal, fate deals a lousy hand from the bottom of the deck."

"We both know how very long I had to wait to get a proposal out of you. We can wait a while longer to do anything about that. I hadn't just been waiting for you to get on bended knee, and it blindsided me when it happened. But I grabbed at it because I've come to love you and your family. So let's focus on *them*. They're in the spotlight right now since they're missing and you don't know where to start looking for them."

"And I don't know where to start looking for them." He gripped the steering wheel more tightly.

"Why don't you pull over for a minute," she said.

He glanced her way but did what she asked. He put the pickup in park but kept the motor running as he turned to look at her.

She didn't know what she would have said if his expression had been hurt puppy or resentful anger. Instead, he looked patient, trusting, which gave her a warm glow inside.

"Look," she said, "you said it yourself. You're more vulnerable than usual. You have some skin in the game. You now care deeply for Maury, Bonnie, the baby, and Tanner. I get that. But can you go back to being the cold, methodical Al who whittled through the filth and effluvia of many a case for the sheriff's department and got to the nub, solving stuff that no one else could?"

His eyes opened wide. Then he looked off into the corner of the truck's cab. Fergie could practically hear the wheels turning and imagined she caught a whiff of heating brimstone.

Suddenly, he sat up straighter, his eyes brightening. "I do know where those Aryans *used* to hang out. Maybe. Just maybe—"

He looked both ways, put the truck in gear, and made a big looping U-turn and hit the gas. "There's no guarantee here."

"I know, but we're doing something. That alone is a step up from driving around aimlessly."

Al drove faster than usual but kept a careful eye on the road, and they both watched for cops since they were no longer active law enforcement.

After half an hour, she looked around as they turned onto a narrower road. "Where are we headed?"

"There was a little out-of-the-way motel almost smack on the Hays County line. It always created a kerfuffle—Sheriff Clayton's word—when anything happened there as to whether our department should respond or theirs."

"And the Aryans were there?"

"Once upon a time. Perhaps they still are. It's worth checking. In fact, it's the only place I know to check for them now that we covered their gun range."

Al turned onto a lane of two ruts, almost overgrown with thick brush crowding the sides and weeds and even some bluebonnets growing up between the ruts.

"We're going here?" Fergie looked around at the density of growth, live oaks with limbs hanging to the ground, and small mountains of prickly pear cacti sticking up in what had long, long ago been a pasture.

The truck wove through a stand of pecan trees just starting to get their full complement of leaves although the bluebonnets were up in waves. She'd opened that conversational can of worms once and had gotten his often-delivered tip about how the last hard frost in Texas wasn't past until the mesquite trees put out their leaves. She'd seen spots of their distinctive chartreuse green along their drive, so she knew spring had, in fact, sprung.

The blocks where a single-wide trailer had once rested stood on a rise ahead of them. The trailer itself had slid down the slope of a hill. One end stuck up like a breaching whale. The front door hung open, with a black maw of the trailer's insides gaping like a scream.

"I take it that this isn't where we're headed."

"Nope. Next spread over."

"I find it intriguing how you seem to know the back way into so many places."

He grinned at her as he turned off the truck's engine and reached for the glove box so that they could get out their pistols. On a whim, Fergie reached for the box of 9mm ammo and shoved it into her back pocket once she was standing outside the truck.

Al waved a hand and took off silently to his left. He waded through some tall buffalo grass that seemed perfect for a rattlesnake ambush. His head was bent forward enough to watch for snakes while following a former trail, pretty much overgrown.

She took a second or two to reflect as they pushed into growth that grew thicker as they entered a copse of woods. One of the things she admired about Al was that he reminded her of something she'd read about Kit Carson. When the Indians had stolen some horses, Kit didn't hesitate. He had hopped onto his horse and said, "Let's go get 'em."

That was Al. When someone took his dog or members of his family, he was off and on the trail without a breath of pause.

Well, hell. They're my family, too, now. Even Maury, the longtime womanizer who used to say to women, "Lay down, I want to tell you a question." All that business about Maury and Al's wife, though painful, was in the distant past. Bonnie got most of the credit for that, and Little Al as well.

Al slowed until he was taking one careful step after the other, trying with each step not to make a crackle or snap. He held up a finger. Fergie knew they were close. When he stopped, she eased up beside him.

Ahead, parts of the back side of an old-time motel were visible. Heaven knew what it was doing way out in that area. It was a little too far from the lake to be a fishing camp. The sky above them was dimming as evening crept toward them, so catching every detail was hard.

The former motel—too dilapidated to still be in business—was comprised of an office building completely open on one side where a wall had collapsed, along with a dozen small standalone cottage-sized rooms.

It couldn't have been much of a motel when it was new. Each building was a hodgepodge of various kinds of stone and brick, some with stretches of worn black tar paper where the stone had fallen away. Red-lettered No Trespassing signs had been hammered into the tar paper with roofing nails.

The area around the motel had grown thick with vegetation, shrubs and vines that had practically crept up to the doors of the cottage rooms. Yet the woods surrounding the motel seemed preternaturally quiet. Not a bird tweeting nor the rustle of a lizard scrambling disturbed the utter calm. Then a scream ripped the silence down the middle.

The door to the end cottage burst open, and a short, squat woman with bouncing curls of blond hair shot through the door and ran across the gravel parking lot.

Two large men came out the door right on her heels, close enough that the first was able to grab her and hold her until the second arrived. They wrestled her to the ground and just as quickly lifted her thrashing body, one carrying her legs and the other with an arm around her neck and one of her arms. She waved her free arm and tried to kick as they hauled her back to the cottage and slammed the door.

"Was that...?"

"It sure looked like Bonnie." Al glanced toward the sky. "Hard to tell in this light."

"What are we going to do?"

"What we have to do." He took his gun out from the small of his back and jacked a shell into the chamber.

Fergie had her gun out. Before they could take the first step, the door opened again, and the two men came out, laughing as they headed away across the lot. Fergie grabbed the back of Al's shirt before he made any noise rushing down to Bonnie's aid.

When his head snapped toward her, his eyes were full of sparks, eager for battle. She pointed down at the retreating men, and he relaxed.

As soon as the men were out of sight and the sound of their boots crunching on gravel had faded, Al and Fergie started down the hill sloping toward the cottage.

Fergie watched each way as they scurried across an open stretch until they were standing at the door of the cabin. A sliding dead bolt locked the door shut from the outside.

She slid the lock open, and Al charged inside.

"Clear," he said.

She followed inside and saw why he could say that so quickly. A single 40-watt bulb hung by its cord from the ceiling. The room was small, with a tiny doorless bathroom in one corner. In another corner, a potbellied iron stove sat like a time visitor from the past. The woman they'd seen was sitting on a straight-backed wooden chair, one wrist handcuffed to the stove.

"You're not Bonnie," Fergie said.

From a distance, the woman had looked like a dead ringer for Bonnie—up close, not so much. Her bouncy blond curls and build had fooled Fergie.

"Actually, my name is Mariana."

Fergie dug out her set of keys from her jeans pocket. She bent close and unlocked the handcuffs. Out of habit, she moved the cuffs to a back pocket.

Mariana had a tan tint to her skin and a round little moon of a face, with a pert, up-tilted nose and eyes with the barest slant to them. *Hard to tell where she's from, except not from Texas.* Fergie helped the woman get to her feet, though she wobbled, and she stood not too much over four feet tall.

"Actually, I came out here to find Jessie."

"He's here?" Fergie asked.

"Somewhere-abouts. Hard to tell, actually, where they buried him."

Fergie glanced toward Al, who was trying to see out through a boarded window. *If this woman says 'actually' one more time.*

The lock on the door slid shut with a hard rasp. The light in the room went out. Someone had thrown the circuit switch.

Al grabbed Fergie and Mariana around their waists at the same time. From the floor, he pulled the iron stove onto its side with a huge, wood-splintering bang.

"What the—"

Before Fergie could finish her question, gunfire broke out and shots came whizzing through the cabin, some zinging in a metal clang off the stove.

"Is that Jessie out there?" Fergie shouted.

"No. I was trying to find where they buried him, actually."

Bullets continued to slam into the cabin.

Please, oh please, don't let the last word I hear be "actually."

Chapter Sixteen

The limo slowed and pulled into a gas station with a convenience store.

"Be right back," Dom said. He got out and lumbered toward the store entrance.

Bonnie glanced across the back seat of the limo, past Patty Belle holding the baby, and caught Maury staring at her. She wondered if he was thinking the same thing she was—if they opened the doors and ran, they could never get clear with Little Al and Patty Belle along. Tanner looked up at her from where he was curled on the floor, perhaps wondering where they were going. *Good question.* She was starting to think they'd jumped out of the pot into the frying pan with these guys.

Still, maybe they *were* friends of Al, along to help. As if reading her mind, Maury sighed and shook his head as he turned to look out his window.

When Dom came back to the car, carrying two bulging white plastic bags, he put them in the trunk.

When he got back into the front passenger seat, Tanner sat up and growled. Bonnie wanted to say, "That's what I was thinking too."

The rest of the ride wove out along back roads where she recognized nothing. Patty Belle's hands were busy with the baby, so she couldn't talk. Maury's face got longer with every mile. He didn't want to talk. Bonnie petted Tanner and looked out her window. She decided to memorize landmarks and hope.

At last, the limo turned and went down a long lane, past what looked like old warehouses, then along a tall fence where she could occasionally see the tops of large machines. Through a brief gap in the fence, she caught a glimpse of backhoes, cranes, and farming equipment as well as construction machinery.

"What do you have in mind?" Cabe said.

"Purley's place will do. He's not due back for a week," Dom said.

Bonnie swallowed hard and looked toward Maury. As quietly as she could, she asked, "Any ideas?"

Dom looked back at them just as Maury was shaking his head. Dom was smiling, but it wasn't a smile Bonnie ever wanted to see on a dark night.

The limo turned and drove through a narrow gap between two warehouses, its sides nearly scraping the walls as they squeezed through. At the other end, there was barely room for the limo to turn before hitting another tall fence. Cabe jockeyed back and forth until he stopped the limo in front of a back door to the warehouse.

Dom unlocked the door and went to get the plastic bags out of the trunk.

Cabe got out and came around to open Bonnie's door, just the way a chauffeur would.

As she got out of the limo, Bonnie took in the metal outer walls of the warehouse, which had no windows. She held Tanner's leash. Patty Belle followed, carrying the baby. Then came Maury, with his eyes open as wide as they ever got.

Inside was a small, windowless apartment, a place where this Purley they'd mentioned could stay. She doubted he lived in the apartment all the time, or he would have been the most depressed person on the planet. A small twin bed, its cover a green army blanket, pressed against the wall near the bathroom door. A worn brown leather couch was snugged against the opposite wall. At the back of the room, a waist-high row of padlocked cabinets covered the whole wall, except where an opening in the middle formed a desk. An Eames chair, the only concession to anything like luxury, sat at the desk, which had no computer, although a top-grade printer was sitting there. The carpet looked an industrial-grade gray until she realized that it was just bare concrete.

Dom placed the plastic bags on the desk. He shared one of his sinister grins as he headed toward the door.

Tanner lunged at his leash and growled openly.

Then the door clanged shut, and they were alone with their thoughts in their new quarters.

As soon as the door closed, Maury went over to it and twisted the knob. "Locked." He looked around and, after peeking into the bathroom, shrugged. "No window there either."

Tanner followed Patty Belle around as she carried Little Al to the bed and put him down. "At least nothing bad has happened to us," Maury said. "Yet. We sure do bounce from one mess to the next."

Bonnie went over to the plastic bags Dom had left on the desk. She called out the items as she took them out of the bag. "One cheap-ass can opener. Six cans of ranch-style beans. Three cans of Alpo. A six-pack of Pepsi."

"Ah. Beans, beans, the musical fruit," Maury said. "The more you eat, the more you toot."

Patty Belle frowned at Bonnie, who signed what Maury had just said. When she finished, the small girl bent forward, laughing.

"We're a jolly crew," Bonnie said to Maury.

He was inspecting the padlocks on the cabinets and opening drawers. "Found the silverware. At least we can eat. No tools, though. Maybe they're inside the cabinets." He gave one of the locks a rattle. "Pretty sturdy stuff."

He crouched closer, examining every aspect of the locked cabinets. "Aha." His face brightened, and he went over to the silverware drawer and took out a butter knife.

Back at the cabinet, he lowered himself again and used the tip of the butter knife as a screwdriver to remove the screws holding the hinges of the metal plates where the padlocks hung.

"Were you up to criminal activity all your life?" Bonnie asked.

"It pays to know a thing or two." He dropped the first of the screws to the floor.

When he had the last of the screws out, the lock, still attached, and two sides of the clasp fell into his hand. He lowered that to the floor and opened the cabinet.

"Anything in there we can use?" Bonnie leaned closer to look inside.

Maury was poking and lifting. "Not unless what we want to do is make really genuine-looking fake green cards. That's what all this stuff is for. This blue paper is the phony document stock. There's a scanner, a typewriter, a laminator, and a cutting board. There's even phony Social Security foundation paper with light blue marbling over a white background. No wonder they kept it locked."

"Well, it's worthless to us." Bonnie let out a hard huff of air.

Tanner's head snapped toward her.

Maury methodically put the hardware back on that cabinet, getting each screw firmly back in place before he moved on to the next cabinet.

When he finally pulled the lock off that one and placed it on the floor, he swung open the doors. "Oh man. Just more paperwork."

"What were you expecting? Board games?" Bonnie peered in over his shoulder.

Maury picked up a few of the paper forms and examined each one. "It's the kind of paperwork you need to make fake deeds and titles for heavy machinery, the kind we saw sitting outside. I'm getting a pretty good idea of what kind of work this Purley did for them."

Bonnie shook her head. "I just wish he'd been a heartier eater or had left tools around we could use to get out of this tin can."

Maury put the lock back on the second cabinet and moved on to the third and final cabinet. It took less time to open because he was getting the hang of butter-knifing his way inside. "Ah," he said when he got it open. "This one at least has two dishes and two bowls. But no stashes of breakfast bars or anything like that. Not even a can of sardines or tuna."

"At least we can eat our beans now without having to share one bowl, including with the dog."

Patty Belle frowned, so Bonnie signed what she had said. The little girl fell over on her side, laughing.

"I'm glad someone is amused at our plight and is having fun," Maury said.

"Oh, give her a break," Bonnie said. "She's cheering me up, and heaven knows I could use a dose of that just now."

"YOU TOOK THEM WHERE?"

"I had to stash them somewhere, and you was in that meeting with them skinheads."

"Did they see anything?

"It's kinda hard not to see stuff once you're there."

"Well, this may be another one of those little things you need to fix."

"Okay," Dom said. "Just don't leave me out to dry the way Fat Solly done."

Chapter Seventeen

Huddled in the complete dark of the cabin, with wood chips and pieces of wall hurtling toward them, they cowered low behind the iron stove. Fergie was pressed against Mariana, with Al's solid arms around both of them, keeping them as close to the floor as possible.

Just like Al to be protecting us while taking greater risks himself. He was going to make a great husband if they lived through the hail of bullets ripping through the wall.

In the first lull of shooting, when those outside were probably reloading, Fergie said, "I'm sorry about this. We're not doing our best at saving you from those men."

"They were actually going to leave me in here, fastened to the stove to die," Mariana said. "How is this worse?"

"Well, it's not really much better," Fergie said.

A shot ricocheted off the stove. Al grunted.

"Are you okay?" she asked, barely hearing herself above the racket of splintering wood as the shooting picked up in earnest again.

In another sudden lull, as those outside shouted to each other in Spanish, she heard cloth ripping. "Are you bleeding?"

"I've cut myself shaving worse than this."

The room was too dark for her to see him wrapping a wound. "Why didn't they just charge in on us?"

"Probably saw we had guns."

"They're going to use up a lot of ammo trying to finish us off this way."

"They probably *have* a lot and don't want to risk getting near us until we're—"

Fergie couldn't tell whether he stopped himself to keep from scaring Mariana or because the shooting had begun again.

His mouth pressed close to her ear. "We've got to try to get out of here. We can't just wait on them to succeed. Stay as low as you can to the ground."

He reached out a hand to pull hers as he started to crawl toward the door, the only way out of the cabin.

She hated to leave the safety of the toppled stove, but Al was right about the inevitability of what would happen if they merely waited.

Fergie tugged Mariana's hand, and they all inched toward the door. She could hear and feel bullets whizzing past just over her head. She pressed even closer to the ground, expecting a bullet to clip her at any second.

Al reached up quickly to unlatch the door then dropped back as bullets slammed into it. When he shoved it open, it took several hits from the fairly steady stream of shots.

He started outside, staying pressed to the ground and veering to his left. Fergie tugged Mariana along, both with faces practically scraping the dirt and bodies pressed as low as they could go. The steady hail of bullets was an unforgiving limbo bar just missing them.

Then the shooting slowed, and she heard shouting, mostly in harsh, commanding English.

"Drop it! Right now!"

The shooting stopped. Her eyes strained to see anything at all in the dark night. Al had stopped moving.

Beams of light swept the area ahead of where they were stretched on the ground. Fergie could make out the figures of the eight or so men who'd been shooting. They were turning in the direction of the approaching lights.

Two of the men turned and started shooting toward the newcomers. Another one spun and ran toward the cabin. Al rose high enough to fire twice, and that man dropped to the ground.

Shots came from the direction of the bobbing lights. Fergie could only make out three sets of lights. The men in the middle shot back in that direction.

She could barely see at all. The approaching lights were getting brighter against the black night, but with shots being fired back and forth in flashes of color, telling who was who was hard. Another of the men in the middle rose and started in their direction. She could see him clearly enough to fire three times at his legs. He stumbled and fell.

The bulk of the group in the middle spun and at once started toward the three oncoming lights, which were nearly up to the remaining men.

"Drop it! Drop it! Drop it!" someone was yelling.

But the running men didn't seem inclined to stop or drop anything. From what she could make out in the fragmented bits of light dancing around, the bunch in the middle outnumbered the three men who'd just arrived with the lights.

"Come on! They need our help," Al yelled to her.

"Stay here," she told Mariana and jumped up. She took aim and dropped one man right away and saw Al get another.

Shooting from the other side took its toll as well, until the remaining few in the middle dropped to the ground, surrendering. The new arrivals rushed toward them, covering them.

She could make out lights on gun barrels as well as headlamps aimed at those on the ground. "On your belly! Hands behind you!" A couple of the men who'd just arrived bent over those on the ground, putting on handcuffs.

"I'd put away your gun," Al whispered loudly to her.

"How do you know?" she said.

"Trust me."

Al dropped back to the ground, and she joined him.

She'd just shoved her gun behind her belt at the small of her back when men came running over, and the beams of their lights fixed on the caravan of Al, Fergie, and Mariana lying on the ground. Fergie blinked, trying to keep her eyes open.

Like Al, she went limp. Someone grabbed her shoulders and held her to the ground. Another patted her down hard. She didn't struggle. She let the men yell at her and yank her arms to her back as they found her gun and got the handcuffs on. Light beams jerked up and around, probing the area around as they got Al and her standing. They were gentler with Mariana.

"Where's Jessie?" one of them asked her.

Mariana shook her head. She was crying too hard to talk.

"Okay. Let's go!" The man holding Fergie shouted even though he was standing right beside her.

In the kaleidoscope of twisting and jerking beams of light, Fergie could see the other guy wasn't being gentle with Al either, even though part of his shirt was torn away and the cloth wrapped around his upper arm.

One man stood over the handcuffed men on the ground, who looked like the ones Fergie had seen chasing Mariana—Latinos maybe, but not all of them seemed to be, not that she'd gotten a clear look at them. The three men in command of the situation all wore black. She could make out white lettering on the men's outfits: ICE.

As they got closer, she recognized the man standing in the middle—Jaime Avila, Al's friend and ICE field office special agent in charge. Although the other two were taller, Jaime exuded command. He was muscular and had the shape of a bullet, a hard and ready .40 caliber. His head was bare, with a close cut, while the others wore ICE ball caps. He had a Sig Sauer P320 in his side holster and held a Heckler & Koch assault rifle mounted with a tactical light pointed down at the handcuffed men on the ground.

"What the hell, Al?" He waved at one of his men. "You can give them back their guns. They gave us a hand when we were outnumbered." He turned back to Al. "Why are you here, of all places, and how have you managed to get yourself wounded?"

"You may have noticed those men were shooting at us." Al nodded toward the men on the ground.

"But why here?"

"Some of the Aryan Brotherhood have made off with my brother, his wife, their child, and my dog."

"Kidnapping is usually Bureau work. But let's get you patched up, and we'll talk. A Special Response Team is on the way. I called for it when I realized what we had here. I came out here expecting to meet with someone else. I didn't know who the hell these guys were firing at. I sure wouldn't have bet on it being you."

Headlights wove toward them, and a large black van, the kind SWAT teams used, pulled up. Men poured out of it as soon as it stopped.

One of them was already hurrying their way with a medic kit.

"Several of the men over this way are down and wounded," Jaime yelled, "but start on this one first." He waved toward Al.

Al sat down on a stump, and the man began to cut away his shirt.

"I could just take it off," Al said. But he was too late.

Fergie moved close and watched as the medic peeled away the makeshift bandage of torn shirt Al had applied in the dark. A bullet had cut a groove just above the triceps and under his shoulder, coming close to the bone and perhaps scraping it. The wound had bled quite a bit and was still bleeding.

Jaime had gone over to supervise the handling of the wounded men. He got the other cuffed ones headed toward the van. After a moment or two, he broke clear of the group of men he was talking with and came back toward them.

"Was this Jessie one of yours?" Al asked.

Jaime glanced toward where Mariana was still crying hard. Two of Jaime's men were trying to calm her, but she was close to being hysterical. Losing someone close and being shot at in the bargain could do that.

Jaime bent closer to Al. "Yeah. He was undercover. But then we didn't hear from him. That's why we're here. I brought along only a couple of men. Didn't expect to walk into a firestorm and find ourselves outnumbered. Thanks again, by the way, for helping turn the odds in our favor. Now, your turn."

"Fergie chipped in too."

Jaime nodded. "These guys aren't cartel, but they're linked—some up-and-coming wannabes. A lot of folks are stepping in, trying to get in on a disrupted revenue stream now that the powers are shifting. We were hoping to get a handle on their affiliation and where they're getting their product. But that doesn't explain why you're here."

"This used to be a place the Aryan Brotherhood used from time to time," Al said. "They were bringing in product and sometimes even making product. This was a meth lab the last time I was here."

Jaime nodded. "The Texas branch of the Aryan Brotherhood had ties to the Gulf and the Juarez cartels. We suspected some human trafficking was going on as well though they haven't been caught at it. You know, my thing is cartels and anything to do with them. I had a chance to tie everything together in a lead back to the source. But that depended on Jessie." He tilted his head, listening to a change in the distant barking of a tracking dog. "Sounds like they've found him—at least where he's buried."

The medic finished wrapping Al's arm wound. He put away the few things he'd used from his kit, got up, and trotted off to where Jaime's men were standing over the wounded men.

Al looked down at what was left of his shirt lying in the dirt.

"What do you know about the cartel scene, Al? I mean lately. As you know, it's subject to rapid changes."

Al nodded to Fergie. "She can lay that info dump on you as well as I can."

"I know that Joaquin 'El Chapo' Guzman is in an American prison," Fergie said. "His Sinaloa cartel has lost ground, but no one is taking them lightly. One of Guzman's sons was arrested in the La Mora neighborhood of Culiacan, Sinaloa, and armored vehicles of cartel men with military-grade weapons swept in and opened fire until the security forces had to let the son go before more people were hurt. Eight people were killed, and the street was littered with burning vehicles when the cartel members left with the son. But I suppose some outfit is taking up any slack—this Mencho guy, maybe?"

Al was reminding Jaime that Fergie played an important part in Al's life and could be as intelligent and informed, something Jaime's slight chauvinistic bent was prone to overlook.

Jaime grinned. "Right, Fergie. The Jalisco New Generation gang is the most ruthless since the fall of the Zetas cartel. These guys leave sometimes fifty bodies at a time in a pile. They kidnap or burn their victims alive in gasoline barrels or make them fight to the death among themselves with sledgehammers. They represent a whole new level of 'not nice' and are headed by Nemesio 'El Mencho' Oseguera, and the DEA has put a ten-million-dollar price on his head. They've pretty much taken over the chemicals coming in from China and other parts of Latin America—the methamphetamine, heroin, and fentanyl. So a lot of the cartels get out of their way and try to do business elsewhere."

"But these guys here, you say they're not cartel?" Fergie asked.

"Nope. Just the usual sort of unlikely puppets who thought they could get rich quick. They're all former or current members of the Texas Syndicate, and as you know, the Zetas cartel hired out this sort and MS-13 gangbangers to do killings and odd jobs for them before. Now that the clout of the Zetas has faded, we don't know this bunch's latest connection at the moment and were hoping Jessie could get that out of them. You know it's all about turf battles these days and who has the most ruthless power at the moment."

"You think they'll talk now?"

"We can hope, but I doubt if we get much out of them. And they're not Aryans, as far as I know."

"Which brings us to our skinhead thugs, the ones who have my friends. I just need to know where they are or might be," Al said.

"Oh, those Aryans. They're a moving target these days, staying in one place only long enough to do some business and move on before what they're doing becomes too obvious."

"You can't help me at all?"

"I'm afraid not. But I can give you a ride to your truck. We found it while doing the perimeter check. I thought you might be about somewhere."

"Yet you let your guys practice origami on me."

"That's just standard procedure. You know how that is. The practice is good for them. And you get a free refresher on how it's done these days. You'll note that I did see that you got your guns back for wherever else your hunt takes you." He held out a hand.

Al didn't even hesitate to reach out and shake it. They'd been together on nights far dicier than the current one.

As they followed Jaime, Fergie noticed that Mariana, who seemed to be cried out for the moment, was just looking down at the ground.

"What about her?" Fergie asked.

Jaime shrugged. "She was going to be collateral damage, and I suppose she is, either way."

"You need a report or some kind of statement from us?" Al asked.

"Probably best if we don't mention you were here at all. You gave us a hand, so I owe you. I think that puts me two favors in your debt. So I'll pretend I didn't see you at all here. You can scoot for wherever you're headed next."

"I wish I knew where that was," Al admitted.

"Good luck finding your family," Jaime said. "From what I recall of your brother Maury, he'll sooner or later make a splash and let you know where he is... if he's alive."

"The ones who took him have every reason to keep him alive... for now." Al turned toward his truck.

"You'll take good care of Mariana?" Fergie asked.

"You can count on it."

As they passed Mariana standing between two of Jaime's men, Fergie called out to her, "Have you ever spoken a sentence where you didn't...?"

Mariana looked up, her puffy red face streaked with wet. "Actually, no," she said.

Fergie shook her head. *Maddening.*

As she walked away, Fergie couldn't recall the young woman ever smiling once. She wondered for a second if she could. But then, she probably had when Jessie was alive. That surely made his loss all the harder.

AL WAITED IN THE TRUCK while Fergie went into the first brightly lit gas station convenience store they spotted.

When she climbed back into the passenger seat and put two Styrofoam cups of coffee in the cupholders, the first thing she pulled out of the bag was a T-shirt that said Willie Nelson for President.

"Really?" He tugged it on, wincing as he worked his injured arm through. She reached over to help him wrestle it into place.

"You should have seen some of the other choices."

He was glad to see her grin after what they'd just been through.

"I have one favor to ask." She turned to look right at him.

"What's that?"

"If I ever, ever use the word 'actually' in a sentence again, I want you to give me a swift kick in the behind."

"Do you want me to start now?"

"Wait until I transgress," she said. "I do feel sorry for that young gal, though. Her life will change over something that may not even do any greater good."

"Let's try to do better." Al eyed the bags she'd put on the floor by her feet.

"I also got you some of your standard road-warrior fare, packets of beef jerky and a couple of Diet Cokes. For myself I got breakfast bars and water as backup."

"We've been on too many of these outings. You know me too well."

"What now?" she asked.

"We seem to hop from one distraction after another when this was supposed to be building up to a big event for you."

"Don't worry. I'm not going to go all Bridezilla on you. And the event, if and when it happens, should be a big one for you too. Are you tired?"

"Of course I am. But as long as we can still generate ideas about how to find Maury, Bonnie, Tanner, and Little Al, we need to keep our feet moving."

She nodded. "Go ahead and tell me what you've got."

"We haven't seen or heard anything from Kemper. Perhaps it's because he knows something."

"You were thinking about that while we were being shot at?"

"Weren't you? I figured you were at least fixated on wedding plans in such idle moments."

"Well, I wasn't. I was thinking it would be nice if we were alive for a few more years, though."

He nodded. "I guess that's what I was thinking too. Let me try something."

Al took out his phone and punched in Victor Kahlon's home number.

Victor didn't answer for a while, and when he did, his voice was an irritated rasp. "Do you have any idea what time it is?"

"Of course I do. Watches still work where I am. I wanted to know if Kemper's men or the Aryans seem to be near my place."

"Unfortunately, no. No one else has tried to get in or set it on fire either."

"They all seem to know more than we do. Are the petty crimes marching on?"

"With increased rapidity."

"I'd give worlds to know how information is being exchanged, but Kemper still doesn't know who is behind the crimes."

"I'd give worlds to sleep one uninterrupted night." Victor hung up.

"Where to now?" Fergie asked.

"We need to find out as much as we can about Kemper Giles, and as quickly as we can."

"So... no rest for us?"

"Not yet."

Chapter Eighteen

Bonnie watched as Maury worked his way along the back wall of their quarters, tapping at it and listening. He stopped when he got to the small bathroom then went inside. She could hear him tapping in there too.

When he didn't come out right away, she asked, "What are you doing?"

"Looking for studs."

"Been there. Let me know if you find any."

"Not that kind. At some point, this room was added to the inside of the warehouse. While the outside looks to be a pretty tough shell, I'm hoping that's not the rule on the inside."

Bonnie got up off the bed from the other side of Little Al, who was sleeping. She stepped around Tanner, lying stretched out at her feet, and signed to Patty Belle that she would be back.

She went over to see what Maury was up to inside the bathroom.

Maury was crouched in the shower with the shower curtain pulled to one side. "You see this?" He pointed at some three-by-three-inch pale-blue tiles running up to about waist high from the base of the shower floor.

She nodded. "What about it?"

"This grout was starting to give way, was going to need to be touched up soon."

"And?"

"It's about our best bet for now. I can hardly go through the wall where those cabinets in the other room are blocking the way."

He tapped at a tile with the thick end of the butter knife he held. The click sounded low and hollow. He moved the knife a few inches to the left and tapped. The click was high and bright.

"Stud," he said.

"How does it help you knowing that?"

"Because I need to know where the studs aren't." He turned the knife around and started digging at the line of white grout around a tile. "This is apt to take a while. You might want to fetch a chair if you want to watch. Or come back in a spell."

She let out a hard huff of air and went back out to join the rest of her crew. But having a notion of what Maury was up to cheered her as she went over to help Patty Belle, who was attempting to change a squirming Little Al on her own.

AL WAS WITHIN A MILE or two of Kemper Giles's home base when he saw Giles's black limo pass him in the other direction.

He eased left into a turnaround that crossed the median strip of grass. After two cars and a pickup went by, he pulled into traffic going the other way. His truck tires rasped as they gripped the asphalt and his truck surged like a hound hard on a hunt.

"Where are you off to now?" Fergie asked.

"Playing a hunch." Al glanced in the rearview mirror. Traffic was pretty clear behind them. He stepped on the gas until he soon glimpsed the limo far ahead.

BONNIE CHECKED ON MAURY a few times as he kept at his task, chipping away in the bathroom for most of the day, pausing only for a shared lunch of beans, then going right back to work.

He'd been at it again only a short spell when Bonnie heard a vehicle pull up outside the door and called out, "Maury, company's coming."

Maury yanked the shower curtain closed and rushed out to join her. "Time to feed the little one, wouldn't you say?"

When the key turned in the lock and the door opened, Dom's hulking figure started to ease into the room. Then he saw Bonnie with a bare breast held up to the baby's grasping mouth, and he stopped where he stood. His eyes widened before he looked away.

"You folks okay?" he asked.

They nodded.

He looked around and backed out the door. The car outside soon started up and pulled away.

"That was clever," Bonnie said. "His eyes were sure fixed elsewhere, and he didn't give the place a very thorough check."

"My eyes were there too." Maury sighed. "Now, back to work."

He trudged back into the bathroom even though his fingers looked tender and a little raw from picking away at the tiles. Bonnie followed closely. He pulled aside the shower curtain, revealing enough removed tiles for Tanner or Little Al to get through, but not the adults yet. He started cutting away chunks of the drywall.

"I'll be able to start pulling away bigger chunks soon or even kick at it a little," he said.

He was looking tired and frustrated enough to enjoy some kicking. Tuckered as he was, Bonnie had never been prouder of him than she was of his sweaty, worn self at the moment.

Bonnie tapped him on the shoulder. When he turned around, she held the baby out to him. "You tend to Little Al for a spell. Patty Belle and I want to take a turn at all the fun you're having. I've figured out what you're up to enough to want to help now. Okay?"

He shared a tired grin and reached out two arms. Holding the baby, he went out into the room and sat on the bed, with Tanner crowding close to his ankles while the two little dwarves set about their task over in the mine he'd started at the back of the shower.

When he peeked in at them later, they'd paused to communicate in sign language. He didn't ask what they were discussing. Working together, they'd been making more progress than he had. He'd left them a pretty good start, though. He went back out into the bigger room.

"Hey!" Bonnie yelled barely an hour later. "You'd better come look. I think we're breaking through to the other side."

Maury rushed back into the tiny, crowded room. Tanner got excited and followed closely. He had only a couple of white patches of gauze and tape left since they'd been able to remove some where he'd been healing. He had patches of thin hair here and there, where it had been cut away and healing scabs showed through.

Bonnie pointed at the growing hole in the wall. Loose tiles lay scattered on the shower floor. The hole on the near side was big enough for a person to duck and get through. Bonnie had cut a black hole the size of a basketball in the second layer of drywall.

"We couldn't see anything on the other side. Both Patty Belle and I stuck our heads through, and it was just too dark."

"Stand aside," Maury said.

Bonnie pressed her back to one side of the shower, and Patty Belle slipped around Maury and Tanner to go out to check on the baby.

Maury was far from being as robust and physically fit as Al, but he reared back and kicked the drywall on the other side as hard as he could. The hole widened.

He kicked and kicked until he had to stop, bent forward, holding his knees and panting.

Bonnie patted him on his damp back then took advantage of his resting to move close and tear at the weakened edges of the hole. "It's nearly big enough for us to get through."

"That's all I needed," Maury panted, "just a little more encouragement."

He moved her aside with a hand to her shoulder and began to kick again.

Piece by piece, the rest of the drywall crumbled and fell away. It hadn't been tiled or even painted on the far side. In just a few more minutes, he'd made a hole big enough for them to get through. The two-by-four wooden studs had been generously spaced twenty-four inches apart instead of the sometimes sixteen inches. The hole reached nearly to each stud—plenty of room.

He was bent over huffing.

Bonnie said, "I'll go round up our stuff, even what's left of the beans, though I wish we could leave them behind. They've done enough harm in the world."

Maury was standing upright when she came back. Bonnie handed him their backpack, which was a little heftier, but he slipped it on. She had Little Al in his papoose on her chest. Holding Tanner's leash, Patty Belle showed no fear but had an eager gleam in her eyes.

Bonnie had just a second or two to reflect that, even with her hare-lip and plain features, Patty Belle could be darn near pretty when she smiled.

"And off we go into another dimension." Maury bent and eased his upper body through the dark hole then stepped cautiously through.

Bonnie reached back to take Patty Belle's hand. She stepped through the hole into the black then stopped. She couldn't see a thing except a dim patch of cement floor lit by the light from the bathroom. Maury had already gone out of sight in the dark.

"Stay where you are!" Maury called out, his words echoing in the huge insides of the warehouse. "I'm going to try something."

She waited for what was probably a minute or two but felt like two hours crawling slowly by.

Click. The warehouse lights came out on. Maury stood on the far side of the warehouse, his hand still on a row of light switches. He must have hit them all. Hanging panels of florescent lights showed rows of farm machines, a backhoe or two, Bobcats, and some industrial-size trucks.

"I never understand on television shows why officers at a crime scene use only their flashlights when they could just flip a light switch." He started to walk back toward them then stopped. "And here's my favorite. Come look at this."

Still holding Patty Belle's hand, Bonnie looked around in awe at all the machines as she walked to where Maury was standing. On the other side of a giant yellow road-scraping Caterpillar, Bonnie saw a jeep—not just any current jeep. It was an olive-green Willys jeep with U.S. Army and an eight-digit number stenciled in white on its hood. Its front windshield was a rectangle of framed glass sticking straight up.

"Isn't it beautiful?" Maury went over to rub its army-green hood.

The jeep had no doors or top, and Bonnie wondered if it even had seat belts.

"What do you have in mind?" she asked.

"It's our escape pod."

"Are the keys in it?"

He bent closer to look. "Nope. But I can hotwire this honey."

He went around to look down into the gas tank. Then he shook the spare gas container. Across the warehouse, near the door, stood a tall metal tank with Gas conveniently painted on its side.

Maury took the detached spare gas can and trotted across the warehouse floor. "You can climb in, make yourselves comfortable."

She sat in the passenger seat, and Patty Belle was in the back, holding onto Tanner when Maury carried back the heavier can. "It had a hand crank." He was practically giggling. "That takes me back a spell. I knew a farmer with one like that, and we used to sneak by and borrow some gas back in my courting and sparking days."

"Borrow?" Bonnie shook her head enough to bounce her blond curls. "And those courting and sparking days are as gone as the dodo... unless it's with me."

He nodded as he poured gas into the jeep's tank. "I know." As soon as he'd fastened the spare gas can back into place, he climbed into the driver's seat and fiddled with some wires along the steering column. "Oh, wait." He got out and slipped underneath the jeep.

Maury slid back out, holding a small electronic device, which he set down on the cement next to the jeep. "Tracking device. A GPS. I remember those Aryans mentioning that all their vehicles had them now."

"You think Kemper and those lowlifes are linked somehow?"

"Of course they are."

"How in cornflake blazes did you figure that out?"

"I don't need to have the detective smarts of Al or Fergie to piece that together. And I'm betting it's all about money. Which makes using their gas all the sweeter."

"Not to mention one of their vehicles."

"There's that too." He rubbed the bare ends of a couple of wires together, and the jeep's engine coughed to life. He shifted gears and drove them over to the warehouse's big door.

"And away we go," said in his best Art Carney voice, and got out to hit the button to open the door.

Chapter Nineteen

Al kept his truck far enough back that even a seasoned ex-con like Dom couldn't spot him on the limo's tail. But as they got away from the wider roads and onto narrow rustic roads that could use a little maintenance, he had to hang back even farther.

He might have missed where the limo turned into the open gate of a fenced-in group of warehouses, but he knew not much road was left ahead. The sheriff's department usually had little reason to prowl and patrol out that far, so it was as good a hiding place for anyone up to some kind of no good as Al could imagine.

"I wonder, if we check, whether this place would even be listed as belonging to Kemper Giles?" He pulled the truck into the thickest copse of woods he could find within a running dash of the front gate.

"You'd get even money from me on that," she said.

They both had a gun in their right hand as they crouched low and scurried along the length of a six-foot-high chain-link fence.

He caught glimpses of a few yellow-and-green machines and for the first time had a clearer inkling about what Kemper Giles was up to with this out-of-the-way property.

Al could only guess at the contents of the warehouses, but he figured he was getting a glimpse of a good-sized operation.

He glanced back toward Fergie. She shook her head, so she hadn't spotted the limo either.

They shot through the open gate and hurried over to cling to a shadow against the metal side of the nearest warehouse.

The warehouses were locked. He figured the limo itself would be the biggest tip-off. They scurried along the edges from one warehouse to another. When he started around the back end of a warehouse near the far back fence, he spotted the parked limo. He held out a hand across Fergie's chest, stopping her.

Al eased backward.

"They're here?" Fergie asked.

"I can only see Kemper's caddie."

He peeked back around the corner just in time to see Cabe and Dom come out the back door of the warehouse and climb into the limo. It pulled quietly away and was soon around a corner and out of sight.

Al rushed along the back of the warehouse, with Fergie right behind him, until he was standing in front of the door. "Locked."

"Should we bang on it?" Fergie asked.

"Maybe we'd better get an idea of what's inside first or who's inside." Al started along that face of the warehouse until he could peek around the corner to see down the longer side. "No windows here either."

He took off at a jog, staying close to the building. Fergie had no trouble keeping up and could, in fact, have passed him easily if she'd wanted.

He stopped and pressed an ear against the building. "Nope. I can't hear a thing here either."

Fergie followed him as he trotted to the far other side, testing the bigger sliding doors and the smaller one. "Locked. Locked." He looked up for windows but saw none, just a shuttered air vent with a steel grate that looked as easy to get through as the gates of Alcatraz.

No one else seemed to be in the area. He'd been grabbing at a thin straw of hope. Al tilted his head and listened. He could hear a couple of grackles cackling and skittering around on the metal roof—other than that, nothing.

He shook his head and went around to the other side. As they started back up that side, Fergie spoke as she ran beside him. "How do you even suspect they're in there?"

"I can't know. I just have a feeling."

"You sure that isn't the jerky and cokes you consumed trying to sumo wrestle each other?" She glanced over at him. "We could try something else."

"I just haven't figured out what that could be yet."

THEY WERE HALFWAY BACK to Kemper Giles's place when Dom said, "Pull over."

Cabe glanced at him but did as he'd asked. "What?"

"Somethin' didn't feel right back there."

"What d'ya mean *feel right*?"

"I mean they were sitting there, staring at me like they were on a stage or somethin'. I don't know. Somethin' was just hinky."

"What do you want to do?"

"Let's go back there."

Dom sat quietly through the whole trip back to the warehouse. He stared ahead at the road while clenching and unclenching his jaw.

As soon as the limo pulled up by the door to Purley's quarters, he hopped out and moved quickly to the door. He unlocked it.

As soon as he stepped inside, he knew something was up, that his suspicions had been right. That damned dog should have been growling at him. It was quiet in the room—far too quiet.

He went back to the door. It seemed okay. They hadn't managed anything with it. He was looking in every corner of the room when Cabe came up beside him. "Where are they?"

"That's what I'm tryin' to figure out. Giles thought it was a bad idea bringing them here, and it's turnin' into a worser one."

Inside the bathroom, he tugged aside the shower curtain and saw the hole in the back wall. "Those bastards."

Cabe was pressing against him as they both rushed to look through the hole. He could hear a motor running. Dom stuck his head through. His shoulders were too wide. The lights were on in the warehouse. He thought he could make out that mousy little guy, Al's brother, at the far end, sliding open one of the big doors.

He clawed at the edges of the hole, ripping away big chunks of what remained. Cabe was doing the same on the other side of the hole, but he pressed into Dom while doing so.

Dom gave him a shove. "Give me a little room here." He started to squeeze through the hole, but it was a tight fit. He gave a brutish shove that would have made any football linesman proud and popped through. He could hear Cabe scrambling through the hole after him.

He ran as flat out as he could go, which felt more like a frantic lumber. As he passed the spot where the jeep had rested, he saw the GPS transmitter lying on the concrete floor.

Ahead, Al's brother hopped into a Willys and popped it into gear, and the jeep shot out the door.

"They're getting away!" he yelled.

"I'm right here beside you." Cabe rumbled to a stop and bent to hold his knees while huffing away.

Dom spun and ran back toward the hole into Purley's quarters. "No time for resting!"

Cabe stood upright and took off as well. Dom squeezed back through the hole with Cabe right after him.

"What about the GPS?" Cabe yelled as they came out the door.

"I saw it on the cement back there. They ditched it."

They ran to the limo and climbed in, and Cabe took off in a flurry of gravel.

FERGIE HAD PASSED AL in their trot back along the side of the warehouse when she saw the limo go past. She heard it stop, and she and Al both dived to the ground. She didn't think they'd been seen.

They listened. She thought she heard the warehouse's small door being unlocked. She eased to her hands and knees and moved that direction. They'd crawled only a few feet when they heard an engine roar.

Behind them, an army-green Willys jeep was throwing gravel as it took off from the other end of the warehouse.

Fergie's head snapped up. "Is that Maury behind the wheel?"

"Looked like it to me, and Bonnie's with them. Tanner's in there too, I think."

They heard the back door to the warehouse slam open against the metal wall.

"What about the GPS?" one of them yelled.

"I saw it on the cement back there. They ditched it," someone with a deeper voice hollered back.

An engine fired up with an eager burst. Then the limo whizzed by as it gave chase.

Al stood. "We'd better get moving." He held out the keys to Fergie, admitting that she had the speed between them.

They both took off as fast as they could go.

Al's steps faded behind her as she opened up her stride into a heading-for-the-finish-line kick.

By the time he came running up to the truck, she had the engine going and the passenger door open. He jumped in and slammed the door, and she took off.

She followed the smaller road to the slightly wider road, the way they'd come in, until she came to the highway. Having to guess, she turned the way she'd last seen the limo.

Al's breathing was back to normal. He fastened his seat belt and settled in for the chase.

They didn't have to go too far before seeing blue and red flashing lights ahead.

"Oh lordy," Fergie said. "I sure hope Maury didn't wreck that jeep."

As they neared the lights, she could make out a Highway Patrol cruiser pulled up behind the Cadillac XTS limo.

"Whew." Al let out a breath he'd been holding. "I'll bet getting a ticket isn't adding to the day Dom's having."

As they passed the stopped limo, Fergie couldn't see the driver's face or Dom's, but she imagined fumes shooting out the ears and nostrils of both.

"Let's pull over and wait," Al said.

Fergie waited until the road's shoulder widened into a patch of gravel big enough that semi rigs could stop there. She put the truck in park.

She glanced toward Al. "Didn't you hear them say that Maury must have gotten rid of a GPS tracker that had been on the jeep?"

He nodded. "I did. That'll help Maury and Bonnie's escape. Now if only *we* can find them."

Ten more minutes went by before the Highway Patrol cruiser passed them. The limo silently swooshed by not long afterward.

Fergie waited a moment and pulled out onto the highway after it. "I can imagine steam shooting out of Dom's ears about now."

"He might have anger issues," Al agreed, "but Cabe seems to have slowed to a steady pace now. Do you think they're headed home, to Kemper Giles's place?"

She was looking in the rearview mirror and saw a flurry of vehicles rapidly approaching.

Al glanced back. Before she could answer, two pickup trucks and three bikers whooshed past with a roar of engines. Those on bikes were easier to see than the ones in trucks.

"You'd better slow up and let these guys do their thing," Al said.

She'd seen at least one swastika, and none of them wore helmets or had any more head hair than a mouse's butt. Fergie had slowed as much as she dared.

In just another mile or so up the road, the limo had pulled over to the side once again, and the trucks and bikes were clustered around it.

Al could make out Dom and Cabe amid a circle of the Aryan Brotherhood members. Everyone seemed to be waving their arms and yelling at each other.

"They seem to know each other," Fergie said.

"But not in an altogether friendly way."

"Nope. I wouldn't call them pals, especially at this moment," she said.

Al nodded, but Fergie was watching the group as they went past.

He turned to look back as the scene passed out of sight. "I must say ol' Dom is certainly having a day of it."

"Want to wait somewhere and see how this sorts out?"

"Nope." He settled into his seat. "I think it's home to the Batcave for us, Alfred, and hope Maury and the others find a way to contact us."

Fergie stepped on the gas and brought the truck up to speed again.

She slowed as they neared the house and went past a ways then back, peering into the woods, before she turned into the lane.

As the trucked rolled up within sight of the house, the Willys jeep was parked behind Fergie's car. She felt a wave of relief that they were okay then started running the permutations of possibilities through her head, none of those too favorable.

Fergie shook her head. "Of all places, why did they come here?"

Chapter Twenty

Fergie was still rolling his truck to a stop in front of the house when Al grabbed his Sig Sauer out of the glove box and was out his door and running toward the front door. She reached over, shut the passenger door, and got her Glock from the same place. Then she locked the truck and headed for the house quickly enough to be right behind Al as he burst through the front door.

"There he is!" Maury jumped up from the couch. "You won't believe—"

Tanner ran toward Al, who did bend to pet him but kept right on going through the room.

"It's gonna have to wait. Come with me." Al ran through the living room toward his bedroom.

Tanner followed, jumping up at Al and pawing at him as they ran.

Bonnie waved from the kitchen, where she was just putting a pot on the stove to boil water. She pointed at a small, pale blond girl standing beside her with dark-rimmed glasses and wearing the baby's papoose on her chest with Little Al in it. "This is Patty Belle. What's—"

"Give Al a second or two," Fergie said. "He's in one of his moods."

When Maury and Al came bustling out of the master bedroom, Maury was carrying Al's shotgun, and Al had his black leather duffel bag full of handy gadgets.

He held out the .30-06 to Bonnie. "You know what to do with this."

"I sure do." She grabbed the rifle, started for the door, stopped long enough to go back and turn off the burner, then spun and ran for the door as fast as her stout legs could take her.

As Maury and Al went out the front door after her, Al was asking, "Do you remember exactly where that GPS tracker was located on the jeep?"

Tanner stood at the closed front door for a minute then spun and trotted over to say howdy to Fergie with a few licks of her hand.

Patty Belle moved her hands.

Fergie shook her head. "No. Sorry."

The girl shrugged then smiled. For the first time, Fergie realized the girl had a harelip but could manage a beautiful and sincere smile. She was quite the little ray of sunshine on what was turning into a day that needed any joy it could get.

Tanner leaned closer against her leg and let Fergie dig her fingers into the fur of his back. He had only a couple of formerly white bandages left. In the spots where his fur had been cut away, his scabs were healing.

The front door opened, and Al stuck his head inside. Tanner went bounding that way. Al kept him inside with one leg. "It's about show time, Fergie."

She waved goodbye to the girl babysitting Little Al and loped across to the door, taking her gun out from behind the small of her back as she did.

"Any idea of what's going on?" she asked as she came up to stand beside him, facing up the drive.

"Maury caught me up on as much as he could in the time we had. Maybe you'd better ease over there to the left and disappear in that thickest brush. But stay close. There'll be a line of fire, but you know where that'll be, so you can stay clear of it."

She glanced up the hill to where Bonnie was probably hiding, though she couldn't see anything. Maury wasn't showing on the other side of the drive, but she figured he was over there somewhere. So she would have to be careful if she needed to shoot in that direction.

They didn't have to wait long. The limo was the first vehicle leading what looked like a caravan of the trucks and motorcycles she'd seen earlier.

Al stood in the center of the drive, waiting for them, his feet spread and his gun in one hand down at his side. She didn't know what he thought in moments like that, but he looked like he'd gone all Gary Cooper in *High Noon*.

The limo stopped just a foot or two from him. The passenger door opened, and Dom stepped out and held the top of the door as he spoke over it. "What the hell's wrong with you, Al? You act like you got the upper hand here or somethin'."

"I think you know what has me upset."

Dom glanced over at the Willys jeep.

A number of the Aryans had gotten out of the trucks or off their bikes. They spread out like a football defensive line around where Dom stood.

"We've just been tryin' to protect you. That's all. Hoping you can do a favor for us."

Peeking through the thick green of the limbs that hid her, Fergie watched the line of Aryans edging forward.

Al called out to one of them, "You there. Bitso Mullen. You know the difference between kidnapping and protecting, don't you?"

A big man in black leathers, who'd been on one of the bikes, shrugged. He and the others took another half step forward. Most had their hands curled into fists, ready to see action, and one or two held guns, in clear violation of their paroles. But Bitso stood out among the lot as someone who had risen to leadership in the dankest of prisons. His face had that quiet sneer of nasty power. He looked eager, and the men around him were stirring for action, which Fergie knew only too well from her years in law enforcement. One by one, they kept inching restlessly forward. She would have given worlds to hear the screaming whine of approaching sirens coming to their rescue, but no such luck.

"You with the ball cap on, next to Bitso!" Al yelled. "Hold the cap in the air."

The man, as big a thug as any of them, glared at Al then looked at Bitso, who gave him a curt one-inch nod. The guy looked back at Al, hesitated, sneered, then did as asked with a defiant stare.

He had barely lifted it above his shoulder when a shot sounded and the cap flew out of his hand. All of them glanced in that direction except the one looking at the hole in his hat on the ground. He was probably wishing he'd raised the hat higher.

Maury chose that moment to fire off a round into the air from the shotgun. Some of them ducked as if expecting pellets.

What the hell. Fergie raised her gun and fired a shot into the sky.

Dom's eyes opened wider as he glanced left and right. The Aryans froze for a moment where they stood.

"You know how this goes!" Al yelled. "The leaders go down first."

Dom glanced toward Bitso, who was looking back at him. Some of the eagerness to leap in and rumble had faded from his face. Dom looked back at Al. "I'm no leader. I'm just a humble servant here."

"Yet you'll be buried like a king."

Dom's shiny pumpkin of a head turned to Al, and he squinted and grinned. "I guess we got one of them... what-do-ya-call-its, a stand-off."

"Not the way I see it," Al said. "You should all go."

"Look, we can protect you, like we was doing—"

"Without being wanted or asked."

"All my boss wants is for you to find out what we asked before. You do that, and we're all square. We forget our little disagreements and walk away then. But we need to take your people with us so we got, you know... leverage."

"Not gonna happen." Each word came out of Al's mouth like celery being bitten.

"And I want the girl back," Bitso said. "She belongs to us."

"That's not gonna happen either. You know better," Al said. "She belongs to no one."

"You gotta bend here with somethin'," Dom said, "or I'll lose face with my boss, and you wouldn't want that, an angry Dom to deal with."

"I've dealt with it before," Al said. "And I wasn't the one who ended up in a private room in public accommodations."

"C'mon, Al. You gotta give me somethin', or this ain't over."

"I'll tell you what I'll do. I'll get after this person and solve your problem. In return, you go away. Leave me and mine alone. Hear?"

"I got your word on that?"

"You've got my word. Do I have your word?"

"Deal."

"Hey, the jeep," Dom said. "It's ours. We take it."

"Okay with me," Al said.

Bitso waved to one of the men who'd been in a truck. He strolled over to the Willys, trying to show some vestige of swagger as he went, and climbed in. The jeep started up and pulled out to head back out the drive.

Dom lowered himself back inside the limo and closed the door without slamming it. The men still standing looked toward Bitso. When he frowned, turned, and started back toward his bike, they followed. The trucks had to back out of the lane, as did the limo. The bikes, easier to turn, headed back the direction they'd come.

Off they went, a small roil of dirt and dust settling on the drive as the jeep brought up the rear in their departure.

Fergie took a deep breath, her first full one in some time, and came out to stand beside Al. "Do you think you can trust him?"

"Hell no." Al grinned. "Not any farther than I can throw him, Cabe, and the limo as well into the lake."

"Yet you're going to do what they've been asking all along?"

"I had to throw Dom a bone of some kind. These kinds of men, the Aryans in particular, have died in savage fights before that didn't need to even happen. Their fuses were already lit when they got here."

Maury came out of the woods grinning, since he'd had a chance to fire the shotgun in the air. Bonnie was taking longer to get back from her sniper's roost.

"So that was just a ruse?" Fergie tilted her head.

"Nope. In our idle moments, while traveling all over hell's half acre in this county, I've had some thoughts about that. I'm about to give Victor a call and set events rolling here."

"Yeah," Fergie said. "Like it's been nothing but sitting on our hands for all of us so far while hoping for something exciting to happen?"

"Ah, come on. Let's go inside." Al put a hand around her back and started for the house. "We still have a lot of stories to hear and some petting of the dog to do."

Back inside, the old place seemed especially cozy. Tanner's tail couldn't quit wagging. Bonnie and the new girl were having a conversation in sign language fast enough to make their hands a blur.

"What's her situation?" Al asked Maury.

"Do you mean is she illegal? Probably. But she has papers."

"Let me see them," Al said.

Bonnie signed to Patty Belle, who dug in her back pocket and handed over a slim artificial leather wallet.

No money was inside. Al took out the green card and looked at it. "Pretty good." He handed it to Fergie. "It could pass for real at most places."

She held it, looked at it closely, and handed it back.

Al gave the girl back her wallet. She put it away and continued signing with Bonnie.

Bonnie nodded. She put an arm around Patty Belle and turned to Fergie. "She says those women there that are made to be with the men are not allowed to have an abortion. That the babies will be sold... for big bucks."

"Ah," Maury said, "men who think Roe versus Wade are just two different ways to cross a stream."

Fergie shook her head. Of course Maury would try to lighten the moment. But, as usual, his effort was more of a turd in the punchbowl. A bubble of rage boiled up inside her. She expected to hear in greater detail all that Bonnie, Maury, and this girl had gone through. But she'd already heard enough to encourage her belief that these Aryans were just evil, hate-filled vermin. She was trying hard not to be judgmental or prejudiced but was failing miserably.

"The big puzzle to me all along has been how someone affects Giles and those Aryans enough for them to want it stopped," she said. "Now, I'm getting an inkling. Maybe the petty crimes threaten in some way to expose what those bad boys are up to."

Al nodded.

Bonnie got a pot of coffee going then pulled a frozen apple pie out of the freezer.

"No way," Fergie said. "That'll take an hour to be ready. I want to climb into bed as soon as I can and sleep until noon."

So Bonnie put it back and got out a half gallon of butter-pecan ice cream.

Fergie's eyebrows shot up. She'd been trying so hard to get the family into a more healthy style of eating. Bonnie must have been doing some shopping on her own.

Patty Belle's eyes lit up, and she started to clap her hands but stopped, not wanting to wake the baby, whose little head leaned against her chest, his eyes closed.

Bonnie signed to the girl, and they went off together, heading downstairs to put Little Al into his crib.

"Are you about ready for bed too?" Fergie asked Al.

He suppressed a grin. "In just a few minutes. First, I need to set the wheels of justice into motion."

He took out his phone and punched in a number. "Yeah, Victor, it's me. Calm down a minute. I've got something for you to sink your teeth into." He waited while Victor talked then gave Fergie an eye roll. "Okay. Here's the thing, though. You know how Clayton thinks I sometimes dance a little too close to skirting rules and such—how I 'work in mysterious ways my wonders to perform'—his words. Well, this is going to be one of those things, the kind that may well give Clayton ulcers the size of longhorns."

After Victor replied again, Al turned on the phone's speaker and said, "Yeah. Yeah. I suspect he secretly enjoys it too. Now I want to ask about Dolores del Rio—"

"She's released," Victor said. "Out on her own after the usual ambulance chaser bustled in to spring her. She went off in quite a huff, though, while sharing some pretty salty language."

"You don't happen to have any of her stuff, like her cell phone, do you?"

"Of course not."

"Okay. I think I can get around that by setting her name into a burner phone's ID."

"Just what the hell do you have in mind?"

"Maybe it's better you don't know, just this moment. I'll explain everything... tomorrow." He gave Fergie a broad wink.

As soon as he put his phone away, he held out a hand and headed for the master bedroom with Fergie.

Maury looked up from where he was scooping ice cream into bowls. "Aren't you sticking around for coffee and such?"

"Nope. Maybe tomorrow," Al said, closing the bedroom door behind him.

He put the guns away and closed the safe while Fergie stood in front of the dresser mirror running a brush through her long red hair, which was going to need a little touching up at the roots. She felt tired to her very bones and had a growing apprehension that they were far from over with all the threats from various directions, but oh my heavens, it felt good to be home again. She could even see an eager twinkle in her own eyes as Al turned back the covers on the bed behind her.

KEMPER GILES SAT BEHIND his desk, pouring an inch and a half of Pappy Van Winkle's Family Reserve over ice cubes in a glass engraved with his initials.

Dom tapped on the open door and came into the office, which looked more like a den. Cabe was right behind him. He stared at the bourbon splashing down on the ice and licked his lips. Dom stared at Kemper with those blank prison eyes of his, which probably made most people in the joint squirm.

"Don't get comfortable," Giles said. "This is going to be a long night for both of you. You know what needs to be done."

"We're enforcers, not staff," Dom said.

"You're also the ones who didn't think or reach out to me first, and now some fixing needs to be done, and done fast." Kemper took a sip from his glass and slowly put it down on a leather coaster.

"You wanna move everything?"

"Everything."

"But—"

"You can use all of the men I can spare and can count on some of Bitso's group to help. But it is going to happen and happen tonight. Capisce?"

"I was just gonna—"

"Fewer words, more action. You're the one who caused the problem. You're the one who's going to fix it."

Dom's mouth closed into a tight line. He turned slowly and led the way back out the door with Cabe as his silent caboose.

Isn't money wonderful? Kemper reached for his glass. *With it, I have more balls than the Harlem Globetrotters.*

Chapter Twenty-One

Al stared through the windshield at the house.

"The longer I sit here, the less sure I am about this," Victor said. "It's some pretty thin soup."

Al turned in the driver's seat of his truck to look back at him. "I had to work fast, grab a little more desperately at a thread than I would have preferred."

"Clayton seems to think you're prone to such leaps into the air."

"Not really. I was slow and steady for the most part."

Fergie was sitting in the front passenger seat, keeping a pair of binoculars fixed on the house. She nodded to herself.

"And had the best record for closing cases in the department," Victor said. "It's why he said I could learn from you. But if he saw us right now, he would positively lay an ostrich egg."

"There's a chance, a good chance, that nothing will come of this at all. We'll have just wasted a little time. But if this pans out..."

"I've asked a couple of the department's older deputies in uniform, ones I could trust, to be in the area, cruising about, just in case. Your so-called family is really in some danger?"

"Dom thinks we all know too much, and he's right. It's just a matter of time before he gets it through that thick skull that he needs to act and act soon. The only thing holding him back is what we're up to now, which he will know about all too soon anyway."

"And the Aryans thought they could just ask for your family back to hold them again for leverage?"

"That's a whole other issue I'll need to address when we get anything like a conclusive response here," Al said.

Victor cleared his throat. "*If* we get any kind of response at all."

"Al's nephew, his dog, his brother, and his sister-in-law were all included in that kidnapping." Fergie didn't lower the binoculars to speak.

"Do you think you can do something about that young girl too?" Al asked. "If and when all this is over."

"Al, I'm sitting here on the brink of either a great step in my career or being busted down to doing patrols in the bumfart corners of this county. Sure, I'll look into what I can do if all this lands butter side up. But we're far from that glorified state just yet."

"Hey, I'm picking up some movement." Fergie lowered the field glasses and handed them to Victor.

"Okay, guys," Al said. "Let's rumble."

Al, Fergie, and Victor slipped out their doors, careful to close them with quiet snicks.

Fergie slowed as she jacked a shell into the chamber of her Glock and lowered it to her side.

"Would you rather stay in the truck and make out while Victor does all the work?" Al asked.

She turned to him, eyebrows arched as high as they could get. "No, I'm fine, even eager. I will say that in all the time I've known you, this is the farthest out a limb I've ever seen you crawl. You're going to be deemed one of the cleverest people alive or possessing incredible dumb luck if this works."

"Yet someone is already arriving at her place." Al followed Victor closely as they eased down a slope, keeping an eye on the end door in a row of run-down condos that probably should have been torn down years before.

The stucco was falling off the building in patches that might have made the place look French to some eyes. Formerly red awnings over the doors had sunned to a faded pink.

"Even if you hadn't told me who lived here, I might have guessed Dolores del Rio," Fergie had said when they first pulled up within sight of her condo.

Victor pointed, indicating they should split up and surround the person easing through the darkest shadows toward Dolores's place.

Al could make out the darker hulking shadow moving almost in slow motion. Victor was in position to cut the guy off before he got to her door. Perhaps the guy saw or heard Victor. He suddenly spun and ran in the opposite direction, right into Fergie.

He made the mistake of trying to shove her to one side as he ran at her. She used the extended arm to her advantage, grabbing his wrist and twisting until that arm was tight behind his back and he was up on his tiptoes.

The guy tried to swing at her with the pistol in his other hand, but Al snatched the gun from him as he rushed over. Victor arrived seconds later with his handcuffs.

As they eased him out of the shadows into a brighter spot from the nearest streetlight, Al handed the pistol, a Colt Woodsman .22 with a silencer, over to Victor. "Looks like our Moriarty went old-school with this jasper." Victor dropped the gun into an evidence bag he took out of a back pocket.

They kept walking the perp up the street so that Dolores wouldn't look out her window and see them.

"Can you keep an eye on him for a sec?" Victor got out his phone and made a call.

In less than ten minutes, a sheriff's department cruiser pulled up, and two deputies got out and took possession of the man. His mouth looked weak, but that didn't mean he couldn't pull a trigger and feel nothing in his hollow insides. His eyes swept over all of them and showed nothing, neither surprise nor despair.

The deputies loaded the guy into the back of the cruiser.

Fergie shook her head as the car pulled away. "That's a guy I thought should have been kept away longer. Farley Backsmith, a guy who fancied himself a hit man, more out of personal weakness than any strength. Possession of a gun by an ex-con like that should make him pretty hard to bail out too."

"Did you send him up?" Al asked.

"A good twenty years ago," she admitted, "but you know the deal to stay away from age-related topics when possible."

"Gotcha," Al said.

"I'll be surprised if we get much from him," Victor said. "But it does point a convincing finger toward someone we can now consider a suspect."

As Victor opened his door and slid into the truck's back seat, Al said, "I wonder how long it'll be before we hear from—"

Victor's phone rang. "Hold that thought, Al." He took out his phone and lifted it to his ear.

FERGIE HAD SEEN SHERIFF Clayton in a feisty, angry mood before, but that was overshadowed by the storm clouds on his face when Victor led Al and Fergie into Clayton's office.

"I had to tell him everything," Victor said. "It was as good as my job if I didn't."

"And I only wish it had been a bit sooner," Clayton said, his already low voice nearly growling.

"I hope you held off on booking Backsmith and putting his name in the system," Al said to Victor.

Victor nodded.

"Do you have any idea of the shitstorm you've kicked up?" Clayton asked.

"Then it's probably just as well we moved forward to stage two before we came here," Al said.

Clayton's head snapped toward Victor first then back to Al. "Would either of you mind describing what that might be?"

Victor cleared his throat, but Al held up a hand. "This one's on me. It was my family—and dog—who was held by the Aryan Brotherhood and then Kemper Giles's men."

"Do you have a shred of proof for what you're saying?"

"Just their word, which is pretty good with me."

"But not so much me. Where are they now?"

"Home. Safe for the moment, but hard to tell how long."

"Where were they being held, if in fact they were?"

"That's in the works too," Al said. "I should have that on a plate real soon, with Victor's help, of course."

"That will depend on whether your friend and my alleged detective deputy, Victor, can dig himself out of this pile of cow droppings by then."

"There's more," Al said.

Clayton turned to Victor. "I warned you, and I warned you."

"Yet you keep asking for Al's unofficial help quite more often than I'd expect of a man with a full department of trained detectives and deputies," Fergie said.

"Well, that's about to end. Now." He turned back to Al. "Just tell me what sort of kerfuffle you have lined up for me next."

"The first step was to use a faked copy of Dolores Del Rio's cell phone to send a threatening message to Bishop Rawley, telling him she knew who was behind the orchestration of petty crimes, who had reached out to her to perform an arson."

"Do you mean district clerk of courts Bishop Rawley, a public official?" He glared at Victor.

"Yep."

"And just how did you come to the conclusion he was the one behind all the petty thefts?"

"In the first place, he had the means. He had every record for those he could use, the ones who'd done jail time and probably needed money and certainly some protection if they got caught while doing the crimes, specific to their past, which he directed."

"And?"

"He was also pissy and unhelpful to me when he didn't need to be that way."

"Do you think the facts that you're not what we could strictly call official and that you once washed him out of being a deputy might have played a part in his attitude?"

"Perhaps. Probably. But he was the best fit, in my head, and I had to act fast, for my family."

"So at best, you had a hunch or intuition, if you prefer."

"The thought crossed my mind, too, at the time," Fergie said. "Here's this guy surrounded by the history of everyone's criminal records, which could be used to advantage in a scheme like this, and he really was being nasty rude—to me as well as Al."

Clayton's large head swung to fix on Fergie. "I had hoped you would be the levelheaded one. But Al's sometime willingness to grasp on the tiniest of threads must have seeped into your pretty head."

"It wasn't that tiny," Al said.

Clayton shook his head. "And you used that as the basis of a tactic a particularly keen lawyer might try to make seem like entrapment?"

"But it worked. He rose to the bait."

"Which was?"

"The text message said she wanted five hundred thousand or she would talk. In a direct cause-and-effect connection, a two-bit hit man, Farley Backsmith, showed up at her home."

"And you went along with this witch hunt?" He glared at Victor.

"The results do show a connection." Victor's voice was low and subdued.

"Which gives you enough to get a search warrant for his house, his files, his computers," Al said. "Right?"

"Wrong. Not for a clerk of courts."

"Which brings us to the next step," Al said. "Dolores sent him another message, this time upping the amount to a million, and for a money drop, not a cash transfer."

Clayton sat back in his chair. His eyes opened wide.

"I think we could have worked backward through money drops and eventually gotten to Rawley that way, and with more hard evidence, if I'd had time," Al said. "But I *didn't* have time. I had to act quickly and accept a little risk."

"A little risk!" Clayton shook his head. "Did Dolores happen to specify a drop site for that kind of money?"

"Yep. The 'sometimes islands,' right by Mansfield Dam on Lake Travis. It offers a wide-open view. From a distance, a mannequin could look just like Dolores."

"Would it now?" Clayton tilted his head.

"If he shows up for that or, more likely, sends someone to tend to Dolores, wouldn't we have enough to search by then?"

"Well, I've got to fault your pronouns on that. You won't be having anything more to do with it, Al. I'm turning this over to Cavander Haley from the district attorney's office. He should have been in on this from the get-go."

"We invited him. He declined," Al said. "He didn't think it was organized crime then."

"Well, you've succeeded in convincing him to take over long enough for a closer look. And frankly, I'd rather it's him than one of my staff if a holy shitstorm comes out of this. You, Al, are out of this now, and you, Victor," Clayton shook his head, "just get back to work. I'm sure you have plenty enough to do. This is Cav's show now."

"What about my family?" Al asked. "Their kidnapping?"

"Are they safe now?"

"For the moment."

"Well, let me know when that changes."

"And if I could steer your department to what could take down Kemper Giles as well as the Aryan Brotherhood?"

"They're both organized crime, as you describe them. That puts them on Cav's plate too. You should share the details with him."

AL AND FERGIE PAUSED in their walk around the outside of St. Luke's on the Lake Episcopal Church in an open area where sunrise services were held on Easter Sundays. From there, they could look down across Lake Travis, from the Mansfield Dam to their right and across to the Oasis restaurant with its tiers and tiers of seating for folks who like to have a margarita while watching the sun set across the water. Hippie Hollow was over on the far side as well, one of the only nudist public parks that Al knew of in all Texas.

A voice came from behind them. "Do you think ol' Clayton was a bit more tetchy than usual?"

They turned their heads.

Victor was walking over and stopped beside them. He, too, glanced down toward the sometimes islands. In drought times, the islands seemed to rise out of the water and form a small mountain range of connected dirt mounds that soon became home to sprouting plants. But in rainy times, when the lake was full, the water rose to obscure them. At the moment, they amounted to one small dome sticking up and a smaller one a few feet away.

"Looks realistic from here," Victor said.

The figure of a woman stood near the center of the island. A small aluminum fishing boat and an anchor line stretched to where the anchor had been shoved into the sand and dirt.

"You're not part of this moment of high drama?" Al asked.

"Nope. I'm just lucky not to be back in uniform and cruising the far edges of the country."

Fergie glanced at her watch. "Won't be long now."

As she spoke, a small V-hull bass boat pulled out of a cove and started across the lake at a slow, no-wake pace. The boat seemed to be heading straight for the island.

A drone of noise grew behind them. Al turned his head and looked up. A helicopter was heading toward them, and in the distance, another was approaching. As soon as the first came nearer, getting louder, Al could read the television station's call letters.

Victor looked up and shook his head. "I knew that dumb SOB would screw the pooch on this. His ego is bigger than this state."

"Well now, Victor, let yourself go a bit, won't you?" Al said. "You do have men standing by at Rawley's home, don't you?"

"You heard Clayton. This is Cav's mess. I certainly hope he *did* put someone on the house, but he was probably too busy making sure the media knew about this moment of high glory so he can run for office one day."

The small boat veered away from the island. Two larger patrol boats pulled out from where they'd been hiding.

"Not much of a chase," Fergie said.

"Nor will they be able to prove much." Victor turned away and started to head off. "The guy can always say he was just out fishing or cruising around."

Victor's phone rang and he answered it. He listened and hung up, slipping the phone back into his pocket.

"Either of you know a Vernon Uhrlich?"

"I do," Fergie said. "He should still be serving time for murder."

"Well, he isn't," Victor said. "He's out on parole. Blame it on prison overcrowding. The deputy I asked to keep me informed says they saw him throw a gun overboard. So divers will go down after that. Good thing it wasn't by the dam. It's over two hundred feet deep there, and some say there are catfish as big as humans swimming around down there."

"Do you think they'll get anything by leaning on him?" Al asked Fergie.

She shook her head. "There are deep-water ocean clams that are chattier. He was like talking to a stone.

Victor waved a hand up toward the second copter, which was then circling the scene below, sending down enough air to put a chop on the water. "But all this on the news will almost certainly spook Rawley. He'll be as gone as last year's Christmas."

Fergie turned to Al. "We'd better get home, pronto!"

He grabbed her hand, and they took off running for his truck. Al let go when she started to pull away. He wasn't going to win any races with her. He would have laughed if his insides weren't clenching into a hard knot of worry.

BISHOP RAWLEY SAT AT his desk, as still as a statue. He looked down at the papers he was holding to break the tension trance. His hands trembled slightly, and he realized he'd picked up and put down the same file at least three times, perhaps more.

He glanced up at the clock on the wall. *It should be over by now.*

His executive assistant, Janelle Adamson, whom he insisted on calling only Miss Adamson though she'd been with him for over twelve years, tilted her head at him as she came in to take the files from his out-box and found none.

She went back out of his office without a word.

One time at a Christmas office party, she'd had enough eggnog to throw her arms around him, tears in her eyes, and had said all manner of foolish things.

He had pushed her gently away, which led to the usual workplace awkwardness. She'd pouted a few days, and they didn't look each other straight in the eyes for about six weeks. Since then, it had been all "Miss Adamson" with him. He hadn't wanted romance with her or anyone. What he wanted was fulfilled from his side hobby, which had been growing into a more gnawing and obsessive passion. He had felt real power for the first time... and he was damned well not going to let that soul-lifting thrill be stilled by any backwoods firebug.

He looked out into the room beyond his door, and everyone was busy. He had to know and took a risk.

Rawley slid open the lower left drawer of his desk and took out his personal laptop. He glanced up again. *Yep.* She was writing, her head fixed on something on her desk. Everyone else was hustling and bustling, especially when they saw him looking out the glass at them.

He slid the laptop onto the desk in front of him, turned it on, and waited, keeping an eye on those outside.

As soon as it was ready, he searched for local breaking news, not expecting much, so he rocked back in his chair when he saw sheriff's department boats chasing down the smaller craft near the sometimes islands, with other media copters circling like airborne sharks.

He turned it off and snapped the computer shut, feeling a patina of sweat on his neck and brow. Always a stickler for looking as neat as possible at work, he reached up to straighten his bow tie.

As he came out of his office, the pallor of his face must have been borderline ghastly.

"Are you okay?" his assistant asked.

"I am... I am feeling a bit under the weather, Miss Adamson. I believe I'll go home a little early unless there's anything dire that needs my attention."

Her eyes had been down, glancing at her wristwatch. She looked back up. "No. I'm sure—"

But he was already moving faster than he should've, his legs functioning stiffly but carrying him out of the building.

Once outside, he paused, stood still, and took deep, gasping breaths.

How is it possible? The woman is a functioning idiot. How did she manage to reach out personally? Unless...

He usually walked to work. His home was barely half a mile from the office. Unless the weather was inclement, he enjoyed the coming and going, not in a hurry to get to a house where he was all alone—where he wanted to be alone.

The parked cars whizzed by and then the trees and open green of a small park. He realized he was walking faster and faster and made himself slow to a stately pace.

Rawley turned a corner and froze. Three Austin Police Department cruisers were in front of his door, lights flashing in blue and red swirls, and people from another darker car got out and ran through his open door.

Everything is in there. My files, the escape money I never expected to use, my passport. They're probably already going through my car and home office.

He turned and walked away, trying to think. He had nothing. He'd never expected to be caught at all but had always supposed any hint of discovery would build slowly, that he would have time to become aware—not an explosion like this.

His fists clenched at his sides. He wanted to punch something, anyone—or to bite or kick. He'd never felt as utterly angry or as helpless as he did at that moment.

Where can I go? Where can I stay? I can't use a credit card. A few things he could use were in his locker at his gym, but he couldn't stay there overnight, and they might even think to check there. He could at least clean out that locker before they thought of it. *And then what? Then what?*

Coming out of the gym, he unzipped a small gym bag and stood beside a sidewalk trash can to jerk out his gym clothes and toss them away. He pawed around the bottom of the bag until he felt the comforting hard metal. He'd never expected to have anyone on his trail, much less to get caught, and he'd been horribly wrong not to have an escape plan.

He slipped the gun into his pocket and threw the gym bag into the trash container as well. But saving a last bullet for himself was no plan at all. He had far too much pride and ego for that. He was getting just an inkling of who was behind everything that had suddenly gone so horribly wrong for him. Rawley took off again with determination even though he wasn't entirely sure where his steps would lead him.

Chapter Twenty-Two

Al had to drive all the way around the lake to get back to his place. Driving straight across would've been much quicker, but no bridge existed, though talk of building one had come up several times—more a dream of property developers than a practical reality.

His hands clenched the wheel hard at ten and two, the way he'd learned to drive, though he'd heard recruits were being trained to grip at nine and three for better cornering and turning.

Fergie gave him only a glance or two while keeping her eyes on the road.

As soon as he started down the lane to his house, his apprehensions grew.

"You fixed his problems, didn't you, by unmasking Rawley?" Fergie asked. "Now Giles doesn't need you, except to keep you—all of us—quiet. Same with the Aryans. That's it, isn't it?"

He nodded.

As soon as he pulled up in front of his house, he put the truck in park but left it running. He was out the door, gun in hand, while Fergie was still undoing her seat belt. But she'd caught up with him once again by the time he opened the door and charged inside.

Tanner was sitting like a sphinx in the middle of the room. He got up slowly and limped over to Al. Al brushed a hand on the dog as he rushed by.

"Clear!"

"Clear!"

They called to each other as they ran from room to room until they had checked every corner and closet of the house.

Al glanced at a note scrawled on a scrap of paper and left on the dining table: "You know how little my word is worth. Your gonna have to come after them. Dom."

"No one's here except Tanner." Al dropped to his knees beside the dog and felt his sides and back. "Someone's kicked him, hard, but I don't think anything's broken."

Fergie bent to look at some blood spatter and a fresh small red pool near the front door. "I think he bit someone."

"Good. I hope he bit them hard." Al got up to put food and water in Tanner's bowls. "Take care of the place until we're back," he told the dog.

He and Fergie ran toward the truck. She was seated and buckled in by the time he closed his door. He took off in a spray of gravel that peppered one end of Fergie's car.

She looked back but didn't complain. "Do you know where you're going?"

"One of two places, and the second I don't know yet."

He got to the end of the drive and surged out onto the main road after only a quick look right and left. Then his cell phone rang. He tugged it out of his pocket as he made the turn.

It was Victor. "Al, I'm here at the place where you gave me directions, and the warehouses and grounds are as empty as my hopes and dreams. There's an oil spot here and there but no machines or anything else like you described."

"They've moved them," Al said. "I'm going to send you the password to my tracking service. It'll triangulate a GPS signal once you get ol' techie Meat Jenkins on it. You'd best take some backup. Get there as fast as you can. Let me know if you come across any hostages, and be careful. For God's sake, be careful! They've got some of my family. I'm going after Giles myself, and no, I won't wait for you. All bets are off."

He hung up.

"Does that take care of the other place you were thinking about?"

"It does," he said.

"They even have Little Al," Fergie said.

"I know."

"He's probably trying to bait us to come after him."

"He's succeeding at that. But he should have been more careful what he wished for."

Fergie reached up to grab the handle above the door, keeping her Glock in her left hand. "How did you know they would move all that stuff?"

"They almost had to since even you and I had been there and seen it."

"And you'd thought ahead about needing to know where they might move it to?"

"I had Maury put my GPS tracker in the jeep before they took it back to wherever they had it before. I got the idea from both the Aryans and Giles's group using them in all their vehicles—a little ironic since most are almost certainly stolen."

She nodded. "So the Aryan Brotherhood has been stealing all kinds of machinery and doing some human trafficking. Giles has somehow made a deal with them, selling the machinery, and has his outfit supplying fake green cards and other documents."

"Right."

"And Rawley was a problem because some of his petty criminals were carrying a few of those fake green cards as well, which might have led to Giles in time, and he had a lot to hide."

"It's not going to be hidden for long."

"Well, I'm just glad it all makes some kind of rough sense to me now. I can focus on worrying about Bonnie, Maury, and the baby."

"You might worry a little about Dom if I get near him."

"He's a pretty big fellow."

"And can fall all the harder."

"You're not going to let Cavander Haley know about this, are you?"

"And have that grandstanding jerk show up with seven media crews that cause our guys to end up as collateral damage? I don't think so."

"I agree." She looked around. "We're not heading toward the warehouse area again, are we?"

"Nope. Victor was already there and is headed for where they moved the stuff. There's only one logical place left for us to check."

KEMPER GILES CAME DOWN the long walk from his two-story house, white with yellow trim, landscaped as nicely as a showpiece. His limo was parked at a low red barn. He peeked inside. A man and a woman with a child in a papoose on her chest were handcuffed to one of the biggest John Deere mowers. He couldn't make out the words they were trying to mumble from behind the silver duct tape across their mouths, nor could he imagine what would happen if that baby needed changing. Both of the woman's hands were handcuffed. Her face was flushed red from struggling, crying, or cussing behind the tape, perhaps all three. The guy just stared, trying to look angry.

Dom and Cabe stood close to them, not saying anything. Cabe's left hand was wrapped in fresh white gauze, with a little red seeping through.

Kemper went over to Dom. "What the hell are you doing? Are you crazy? I said to get rid of them. The whole point of taking all night to move those machines and everything was so what little they knew meant nothing."

"You heard from Sarrison. The sheriff's department still know nothin' 'bout you... yet," Dom said.

I should have never hired an oaf like this as an enforcer. Kemper thought it but kept his thoughts to himself. He would face how to deal with Dom once the other loose ends were eliminated from the equation.

Kemper waved a hand for Dom to follow. Once outside, he asked softly, "Why? We don't want anything to lead anyone here. Why didn't you kill them there?"

"I needed bait to lure that blasted Quinn. They weren't to home, and them two ex-cops know stuff too. At least no one's listened to them yet. It's still somethin' we can fix. I'm gonna head over to the location at the old warehouses, where we had everything stored before we moved it, and I'll wait for him there. That's where he'll expect us to be holding them."

"Us?"

Kemper let out a hard breath of air. He was used to having the firm hand, being the boss. This lummox, Dom, had been gradually challenging that authority. He was definitely, definitely going to have to go.

"Just make sure you do the job all the way this time." Kemper paused for a moment. "What if they come here?"

"That ain't gonna happen. Besides, you got half a dozen workers here. I saw that two or three of them were each carrying a gun for the day. Take off on your own for a spell if you want."

"I don't think so."

"It's your call." Dom and Cabe ambled over to the limo, got in, and drove away.

Kemper stood still and stared after them. His hands curled into fists. "You'd damn well better be right."

He waved over one of his men, Jackson, the foreman of the few landscaping workers stuck at the house and made to act as ad hoc guards.

Jackson came over, carrying a single-shot .22 rifle, and frowned. "I dint sign on for none of this," he said. "But I work for you Mister Giles, and I'll get 'er done."

"Just do the best you can. I doubt anything will come our way. But if it does—"

"I gotcha, boss." Jackson grinned like a redneck who'd just found the corn liquor in the hayloft. "I ain't no stranger to occasional violence." His grin revealed two upper teeth were missing, probably from some bar fight or other. He turned and went into the barn.

Kemper glanced at the barn, shook himself, and hiked back up the hill toward the house. Getting everything going smoothly and profitably had taken him years. Not for the first time, he pondered how easy upsetting all that might be.

He kicked at a flower along the path and kept walking.

AL SAW THE LIMO COMING from a few miles away. He pulled over and eased behind a big pink square pillar of granite, one of two on either side of an arch leading back into some rancher's spread. It was the ranch of a cowman who claimed to be the first to bring black Angus into Texas, although why anyone would want to put a black cow in an environment of one-hundred-degree sunny days was beyond Al.

Once the limo rolled past and disappeared over the next hill, Al eased out onto the road again. He knew he couldn't just drive up to the front door. He looked around for a place to park and slip onto the property. Giles's place, as well as those on either side of it, had been landscaped into impeccable models of how an estate should look. They were showcases, advertisements for his legitimate services.

The two properties on the other side of the road were quite the opposite, as though they'd been left to run down just for the stark contrast of it. Between them, a copse of woods ran along a creek, and those trees looked like the best he would find. That would have to do.

When no vehicles were in sight in either direction, he swung his truck across the road and eased into a two-rut dirt road running a short ways into the thickest of the growth. He heard the crunch of shells as he got out of the truck.

Fergie looked down then up. "Pecan trees."

The trunks of the trees were huge, hundreds of years old. Al always liked to think of trees that big being around when the Comanche and Kiowa Indians were still roaming the area.

They both checked their pistols, her Glock and his Sig Sauer, then slipped them inside the backs of their belts. They didn't need to be stealthy as they eased their way to the edge of the road, but old habits prevailed, and they tried not to rustle the dry leaves or step on any twigs.

When the road was clear, they sprinted across and onto Giles's property, which was lined by a white picket fence made of some artificial material and was meant to make the place look like a Kentucky horse ranch. The grounds were mowed, the bushes trimmed, and someone had even trimmed some bushes into topiary balls.

Because the place was that well kempt, it had no places to hide as they approached. Al figured he'd start looking in the barn, which made more sense than the house. They were still fifty yards from the building when one of the hands stepped outside and saw them. He yelled back inside the building.

Al and Fergie ran faster, straight at the man who'd spotted them. He disappeared for a moment then stepped outside again with a heavy rake. In a moment, two more men came out. One held a shovel, the other a hoe.

Al was nearly to the barn when one more fellow came out. That one held a rifle, one Al had seen many times in his youth. It was a single-shot model just like the first one he'd owned. The coverall-wearing man holding it started to raise it. Al ran faster, throwing in some zigs and zags. He could see the barrel jerk left then right. Aiming a rifle at a moving target was wicked hard. Just before he expected the man to pull the trigger, he dove to the ground and did a forward somersault, wishing for a fleeting second that his old high school gym teacher could see him.

The man fired, and the bullet went by but didn't hit Al. While the guy was digging frantically in his pocket for another bullet, like some version of Barney Fife, Al charged him, coming up inside the man's hold on the rifle. He headbutted him with a satisfying *thonk* as his forehead smashed into the man's face.

Al grabbed the rifle as it fell. As the man reeled back, hands going toward his head, Al swung the gun by its barrel and hit the guy in his stomach. That folded him over as he sank to his knees, his open mouth showing a gap where he used to have upper teeth.

The man with the hoe swung it at Al's head.

Al held the rifle by both ends and blocked the blow then twisted the hoe out of the guy's hands. Al tapped the side of that man's head with the butt of the rifle, and the fellow collapsed, dropping the hoe.

Al caught the falling hoe in midair and tossed it to Fergie. She held one end of it high and ran toward the guy with the shovel, but he dropped it and turned to run. He just wasn't cut out for that sort of thing.

With the limited resistance out of their way, they rushed into the barn. At once, Al spotted Maury and Bonnie, whose yelling intensified behind their taped mouths.

"Down!" he yelled, knocking Fergie to the barn's cement floor.

He spun. Another man in the coveralls that seemed to be the landscapers' uniform held a gun, an automatic pistol.

Al aimed at the man's thigh and squeezed off a shot. The man's gun clattered to the floor as the guy fell while screaming and grabbing his leg. The guy was probably just out of his element of planting and mowing, but Al sure wished he would quit screaming and thrashing around while clutching at his wound.

Fergie ran to Bonnie and used her handcuff key to free her. While Fergie rushed to Maury, Bonnie went over to the screaming man, took the duct tape off her mouth, and stretched it across his. When he went to rip it off, Al stepped in and held the guy's hands behind his back.

"Get some of that heavy twine." He nodded toward a shelf along the wall holding different types and sizes of cord and rope, as well as silver spools of duct tape, the kind used on Bonnie and Maury.

Bonnie grabbed one of the silver spools. While Al held him, she taped his wrists behind him and then his ankles while Al held those together. In an act of not-so-tender kindness, she tore off long strips of the tape and taped the guy's leg where he'd been shot. At least he probably wouldn't bleed out.

Maury was rubbing his wrists as he came over to check on Little Al in his papoose.

"He's doing fine," Bonnie panted as she stood up. "Better than I am."

"Where's Patty Belle?" Fergie asked.

"They gave her away. To those Aryans, like she was some kind of slave or piece of property. If I get my hands—"

"Hold that thought, Bonnie." Al was looking out the barn's door.

Kemper Giles was standing beside his house up the hill. He held a cell phone in one hand and what looked like an AR-15 in the other.

"Feel up to one of your Annie Oakley moments, Bonnie?"

"She says she can shoot the eyelashes off a flea at a hundred yards," Maury said.

"And leave him with just enough of a scar to render him quizzical," she said.

THEIR ROUTE TO THE warehouses that had held all the stolen equipment took Dom and Cabe past where they'd moved all the stuff. Dom didn't care for what he was seeing ahead.

"Pull over," Dom said.

Cabe did so.

A couple of sheriff's department cruisers with red and blue lights flashing were parked behind an unmarked car outside the new location.

"How the hell did they find this place? We spent all night moving every damn thing. *Everything!*"

His phone rang.

"Your guy. He's on the property here. Get back here as fast as you can!" Kemper yelled.

The phone went dead.

Dom tried to call back but got no answer. He tried again—nothing.

As Cabe, his one hand wrapped in white gauze, turned the limo around, Dom said, "I wonder why Sarrison didn't tip us off about any of this."

"Do you think we oughta just take off into the high hills or something?"

"Naw. We owe Kemper, and besides, I'd kinda like a go at that smartass ex-detective and his string-bean pal."

"She did push me into the damned water, and their dog bit me."

AL STEPPED OUTSIDE the barn and scooped up the single-shot rifle lying in the dirt barnyard and the one hollow-point .22 bullet the guy had been trying to load. He handed them to Bonnie, who loaded the bullet just as Kemper Giles dropped his cell phone to the grass and lifted his gun to aim it at them.

Bonnie fired.

Giles dropped the gun and grabbed his upper right arm with his left hand. "What the hell? You shot me!"

Such was the man's audacity that he thought it okay to shoot them, but not the other way around. Al shook his head as he and Fergie started up the hill to fetch the yelling man and lead him down to the barn.

None of the other landscape workers had stuck around. The only sound was his yelling as they frog-marched him down the hill.

"You have no idea who you're messing with! I'll have you for trespassing, assault, and anything else I can think up as soon as the law gets here."

"Oh, the law is coming," Fergie said. "But you're not going to like what happens then."

A few minutes later, Al and Fergie finished handcuffing each of Kemper Giles's wrists and ankles to beams beneath the loft so that he hung there facedown, wriggling to no avail and unable to yell past a strip of tape across his mouth.

Bonnie, a nurse to the end, wrapped silver duct tape around where she'd shot him.

"Now, let's get out of here," Al said when she was done.

"Not so fast, hotshot." Dom stood in the barn doorway. He glanced toward where Kemper Giles was hanging and shook his big dome of a head.

He held an inch-thick piece of steel rebar two feet long, just the sort of thing to have under a driver's seat in the event of having to deal with someone else's road rage... or to express it. Cabe stood beside him, holding a pistol in his good hand. The other hand was wrapped in white gauze. Al was close enough to see the gun was a Colt Python .357 Magnum with an eight-inch nickel-plated vented-rib barrel—hard to miss anything with that from the short distance separating them. Cabe started to raise the gun to point it at Al.

"Are you the SOB who kicked my dog?" Al yelled.

"The damned thing bit me."

Al raised his hand faster and shot Cabe in the left knee. "I wish he'd bitten your head off."

Cabe dropped the pistol, which clattered on the cement, and crumpled beside it, screaming.

"That wasn't very fair," Dom said. "You know I can't carry." He could barely be heard above Cabe's screaming.

Al slipped his gun into the small of his back again. "Tell you what. I'll play your brick-head game." He went over to a counter and picked up a new ax handle leaning against it.

Dom took a couple of slow steps toward him, an eager, sinister smile forming on his large squinting egg of a face. He had to step around Cabe, who was rolling from side to side on the concrete and hadn't stopped screaming.

Al didn't wait for Dom. He lowered his head and ran toward him.

Dom stopped and straightened up, looking startled.

As soon as Al was nearly to him, Dom raised his steel bar to swing it down at Al.

Al held the ax handle by one end and poked the other at Dom's eyes.

The big guy's head snapped back.

Al brought the ax handle down as hard as he could swing it onto Dom's right shin. Without a pause, he followed through in a sweep that lifted the handle high again and swept down on the left shin.

Dom dropped his steel rebar with a metallic clatter and bent forward.

Al had already swept behind him and slammed the ax handle hard against the back of Dom's knees.

Dom toppled backward. As he fell, Al clipped him hard on the side of his big pumpkin head with a thud that sounded like ripe fruit.

The back of Dom's head thudded again as he came to rest on the concrete. His eyes were closed, and he looked far from ready for a re-match.

Bonnie rushed in with the roll of duct tape, firmly binding ankles and wrists and putting another strip across Dom's mouth. While she was down there, she felt his neck for a pulse and nodded. He was alive.

"I guess it's true what they say about the bigger they are," she said.

Al, Fergie, and Maury had subdued Cabe with his arms behind his back by the time Bonnie came scurrying over with the tape. The first piece went across his mouth to stop his blasted screaming. Then she bound his wrists. She wrapped some of the tape around his bleeding knee, too, before she did his ankles.

"What now?" Maury asked as he stood and stretched his back.

"Why, Patty Belle, of course," Bonnie said. "We can't leave her in the hands of those Nazis."

Maury nodded. "Sure. Sure. I remember how to get back to that place."

"If that motel is the one I thought of when you described it," Al said, "I've been there a number of times in the past during its various iterations as one form of sin center or another."

"You make the life of a city detective seem dull sometimes." Fergie looked around, making sure no one else wanted a go at them.

All the other hands had made themselves as scarce as good intentions at a Klan rally.

As they climbed into Al's truck, Maury and Bonnie getting into the back seat, Maury asked, "How's Tanner? You mentioned that someone kicked him?"

"And that person is currently ever so damned sorry now for doing so," Fergie muttered.

"He's going to need to see the vet again," Al said. "But he'll keep. Patty Belle tops the agenda for now."

He started the truck, and they were off, keeping under the speed limit, but barely.

Al's phone rang, and he tugged it out. "What's up, Victor?"

"Do you happen to know where Kemper Giles is at the moment?"

"You might check his home and business," Al said. "He's probably hanging around there somewhere."

Chapter Twenty-Three

Having Maury, Bonnie, and Little Al in the back seat felt good, but Al wished he could drop them off at home first to avoid any risk where he was headed.

As soon as they described the motel earlier, he'd known where it was. He'd closed it down when it had been a center for illegal poker games and again when it had been a crack house. Knowing it was full of working hookers who had little choice didn't surprise him. He did wonder if it would still be operating. Places like that had to move often and let their clientele know where, since cruising deputies and word of mouth would reveal their existence sooner or later.

"Do you think Tanner biting Cabe's guitar-playing hand is what made him mad enough to kick Tanner and then pack heat like that?" Maury asked.

"I hope he regrets everything," Fergie said, "and he certainly won't be doing any clog dancing soon."

"That was some handy work with that ax handle," Maury said. "Where did you ever learn that?"

"Tell them, Fergie," Al said.

"It's one of the first things they teach you at a police academy about how to use a nightstick. Lead toward the eyes, which will make almost anyone flinch, and then go for the legs."

Bonnie moved her head closer to the front seat. "A real fight usually isn't like anything most people have seen on TV or expect, is it, Al?"

He grinned, playing back a memory. "One of my first real bar fights happened when I was overseas. I was with a buddy, a medic we called Doc. He and I were sitting in a booth of some dance hall dive when a bar fight broke out. People were throwing fists and chairs. A couple of guys were wrestling with each other as they went past our booth. Without a word, Doc held his long-neck beer by its handle and bopped one of the guys on the side of the head with it as they went past. Beer shot up the length of Doc's arm, but the bottle didn't break. Doc said, 'It's nothing like in the movies, is it?' But my biggest memory from that frolic was one of our guys, Lazlo Hurley, standing by the bar like the Colossus of Rhodes. He was a huge fellow who'd played football and wrestled and was the only one in our company able to bench-press over five hundred pounds. The fight was going right around him while he stood there sipping his beer. I saw one of our smallest guys, Little Warner, go over and get as close as he could and talk with Lazlo—in the eye of the storm, so to speak—while the out-and-out brawl flowed around them."

"You just sat there and didn't get involved in the brawl?" Maury asked.

Al's hands squeezed the steering wheel tighter. "Yep. There was no reason. Some people enjoy fighting for its own sake. I'm not one of them. I need a damn good reason."

"Yet you'll leap right in if there's a reason," Bonnie said, "someone you're defending."

He nodded. "It's the same reason I was in the military—not to be a brawler but to do something that needed doing."

"I sure hope it doesn't come to fisticuffs with these guys from the Aryan Brotherhood," Fergie said. "I've heard tales from prisons that would make anyone's hair stand on end."

Al didn't say anything to that. He kept his mouth tightly closed the rest of the way and thought as he drove. He was heading toward some very bad dudes indeed.

The Aryan Brotherhood, as even Cav had admitted, *were* involved in organized crime, the very definition of a second-generation gang that had shifted away from protecting their turf and committing petty crimes to engaging in larger-scale activities like drugs and, even worse, human trafficking. That was what made Kemper Giles's association with them so heinous.

"Is there anything we'll be able to do?" Bonnie asked. "Patty Belle is our friend."

"I could pose as a potential customer," Maury said, "except they don't usually start accepting those until after five, and we're a couple of hours away from that."

"I want you two to stay in the truck with the baby. Fergie and I will have to do this."

"But we're the ones who know our way around inside," Bonnie said. "A little. But we don't even know where Patty Belle's room is or where they might be keeping her. I sure hope they aren't making her turn tricks or anything."

"She's not... the sort who would stand for that," Maury said.

Al suspected he was going to say "pretty enough," but sitting within backhand range of Bonnie might've changed his mind. Al had only seen the girl briefly, but he was already convinced of her inner beauty and warmth. Bonnie sure treated her like part of the family. *Family.* Al couldn't believe his one-time expectation to live out his retirement years alone had shifted so drastically, and here they were on a mission to rescue yet another budding member.

"Whatever in the world makes you the kind of person you are, Al, to stick your neck out and leap in the way you do?" Bonnie asked. "Though I do appreciate you trying to make a difference."

"I think the phrase 'make a difference' has been overused to the point of making it cliché," he said. "It lacks punch. All I'm trying to do is defend the ones I love. I didn't expect to have the whole herd of you, but since you're around, I'm going to do all I can to keep you around."

"Not to mention you not being able to resist being drawn into fixing anything bad that needs to be figured out—any situation that has a bit of mystery to it," Fergie said.

Al's eyes narrowed. "Here's the mystery in life. Sometimes, stuff just rears its misshapen head. In the course of trying to ignore whatever it is—or downplaying it so it doesn't stress or otherwise annoy you—it grows into something bigger, which may just be able to take your cork under, as well as the corks of those around you."

"You know, we have these little talks and then go get shot at." Fergie shook her head. "But I have to agree here that if we turned this over to anyone else, little Patty Belle could easily wind up dead in the process. But this *is* one especially difficult challenge."

"The place is like a fortress," Maury said. "You can only get in through the front door, and there are guards in the hallways, and you don't know where to look for her. Sounds impossible."

Al felt a grin spreading across his face.

Fergie noticed it. "What in the world are you thinking?"

"There could always be a fire drill," he said.

His phone rang. He glanced at it. "Victor. He probably wants one or two things explained." Al turned off the phone. "We'd better run silent for a while."

"Al, I wish you'd wipe that smile off your face and not treat this like it's going to be a lark. These are dangerous men and almost every one of them an ex-con."

"You would think it would make them less apt to carry guns," Al said, "since that would violate parole for most of them."

"More prone to try to stomp people to death with their hobnailed boots?" Fergie rubbed her forehead. "But I'd bet even money—or better—that anyone doing major theft, probably drugs, and in this case, human trafficking is darn well going to have a cache of serious weapons. We saw some of them practicing at their homemade rifle range. These guys may not be prone to carry publicly, but they are toxic and probably armed to their back teeth."

"We didn't find them pleasant at all when we were guests there," Maury said.

"And the food was nothing to brag about." Bonnie felt at the sleeping baby to see if he needed to be changed.

"Laugh if you want, you guys," Fergie said, "but this is a foolhardy thing we're doing, which I suspect makes it all that much more of a treat for Al."

"It's nice that you and Fergie care the way Maury and I do for each other," Bonnie said, "but—"

"At least you aren't finishing each other's sentences yet." Maury reached to lift Little Al out of his papoose so he could hold him and give Bonnie a break.

"Okay, kiddies," Al said, "we're as close as I'm going to go. I'm going to tuck the truck into as good a hiding place as I can find. I wish I could leave you with one of the guns, but—"

"We can always use this." Bonnie reached into the bottom of the baby papoose and pulled out a silver pistol, Cabe's .357 Colt Python. "It was just lying around back there, so I brought it along. These skinheads still have my Chief's Special peashooter. It's only fair."

"Good heavens. You've been lugging that thing around with the baby snuggled up against it?" Fergie had turned all the way around to stare at Bonnie.

"Maybe he'll grow up to think he's a son of a gun," Maury said.

"Well, his father's sure enough a pistol," Bonnie said.

Al spotted a stretch of thinner growth in the woods to their right and steered the truck off the road, going back a ways into the woods, where they wouldn't be spotted.

He hopped out, cut a couple of low bushes, and covered the spot where the truck had left the road.

Fergie was out of the truck when he came back. They started off through the woods toward the motel.

back of his hand came back smeared red. It probably looked a ghastly mess as well, but neither Fergie nor Patty Belle could give him a hard time about it. The knees of Fergie's jeans, like his own, had torn open, and both had skinned knees and elbows where the rough asphalt had sanded them in their diving around.

He felt one or two stings that might've been bullets grazing him but not making solid hits. Once, he heard an "umpf" from Fergie. But she didn't let up on her vigilance.

Al caught a glimpse of someone scurrying in zigs and zags toward them. It was Bitso Mullen himself, probably showing his men how to lead. Trying to shoot at him while he danced his fandango on the way would waste ammo. He waited until Bitso got all the way to the other side of their defensive barrier. Al peeked under the truck beside him until he saw the feet of the lead Aryan trying to sneak around its side to get to them. Then he fired a shot at the leg he could see. A satisfying scream came from the other side.

Bitso started to pull away from the trucks. Al let him go. He was hardly worth a bullet, with so many others still firing.

More men were coming back out of the motel, and an absolute fusillade of bullets hammered into the vehicles. As the tires of one truck were shot out, it collapsed to the ground. The trucks were never again going to be much use to anyone. Even some of the motorcycles were taking hits, but the Aryans didn't seem to care. The frenzy of battle was upon them. Years of hating everyone who wasn't just like them had formed quite a collective rage.

Patty Belle was crouched into a small huddle with her hands over her head. Fergie kept one arm around her.

She twisted and fired at one of the men who tried to run at them from behind.

More and more men added to the shooting until the sound became a fury of noise—a hurricane of lead, shots ricocheting off metal and asphalt.

Al looked toward Fergie. "Have you been keeping count?" He had
to shout.

"Yeah. I have two shots left." She tried to smile. "Might have to re-
think those wedding plans."

Another pair of feet came running their way. Al rose, fired, and
dropped to the ground again. Though the guy had tumbled, Al had
used his last bullet. He looked at where the nearest gun had fallen and
considered his odds of trying to retrieve it. *Not good*, he figured. *Not
good at all.*

That some of the Brotherhood's number had fallen and lay scattered on the ground didn't seem to slow them at all. Rather, it intensified their fury and effort to empty all their guns until Al, Fergie, and
Patty Belle were dead.

Al reached over Patty Belle and put an arm around Fergie. She
looked into his eyes. Hers grew moist. Nothing was left to say even if
they could have heard anything over the unrelenting din of gunfire and
denting metal.

They'd had those little moments before, expecting to die in the next
few moments and facing the inevitability of it. But this was as bad as it
had ever gotten, and even imagining any kind of hope seemed impossible.

Then Al heard a sound he'd never expected. Someone with a bullhorn was saying to quit shooting and put down the guns. At first, he
thought it a ploy by the Brotherhood. But it was a female voice.

The shooting slowed, becoming uncertain.

Al took a quick peek around a pretty battered truck to look in the
direction of the bullhorn. He caught a glimpse of a line of men in camouflage staying low and running from that direction. They all carried
black assault weapons.

The Aryans spun and fired but almost immediately took serious
losses. The women who hadn't already done so dropped to the ground,
screaming. Some men and women ran back toward the motel. But

more of the camouflaged SWAT team poured out of the doors there, cutting them off.

"Now!" Al said.

Fergie and Patty Belle jumped to their feet with him, and all three ran toward the woods. Fergie glanced backward and fired a shot at someone. Another Aryan appeared ahead, but Al held an empty gun. But Fergie had turned back to look forward and saw the guy. She fired, and he tumbled. That was her last bullet.

They burst into the woods, which was thicker at first but soon thinned out under a canopy of upper limbs that crossed above and slowed the growth of low brush, bushes, and weeds below.

They were making better time than Al had hoped. Each time he glanced behind them, he didn't see anyone. Fergie was limping slightly, with blood seeping from a wound on her upper left thigh.

"How bad is that?"

"Just a through-and-through," she said. "Nothing as bad as you took. You look like the last chapter of *What's the Use*. I think you were hit or cut in half a dozen places."

Al glanced at Patty Belle, relieved to see she'd come through without a bump or a scratch. They'd done their job.

He heard a rustle and looked ahead. Three men in camouflage had spaced out and were holding weapons pointed at them.

They all slowed to a walk. Al and Fergie put down their empty guns and raised their hands in the air. Patty Belle looked at them and did the same, raising her hands while almost giggling, as if they were playing a game.

Chapter Twenty-Five

The men in camo came up to them, and one held out a hand. Al was the first to figure out what he wanted. He fished out his badge and ID, which would mean little to a crook but showed he was a retired sheriff's department detective. Fergie caught on and dug out the badge she'd carried while working for the Austin PD.

The man nearest them picked up their guns, one by one, and handed them back once he checked and found them empty.

"She said to expect you two." The lead guy glanced toward Patty Belle then shrugged. He spoke into the mic on his front shoulder. "They're here."

"She?" Fergie asked.

"Yeah. I guess you both know her, Danielle Cassidy. She's heading up this rodeo."

Al imagined her as he'd last seen her, wearing a black bulletproof FBI vest and a gun at her hip, long blond hair in a bun on the back of her head. Her white blouse and black pants would differ from the others' gear, but she would clearly be in charge. They'd met before. Cassidy headed a human trafficking investigation out of the Houston office. She'd taken over a case they'd been in the middle of once before, but at a good time. Fergie once hinted to Al that she thought Cassidy was slightly ahead on her estrogen tablets. She was making a big name for herself in the Bureau, so Al could see her leaping at an opportunity like this.

Al reached up to feel his head, which still throbbed and felt like it was bleeding. "How did she know I might be here?"

"Your sheriff called Richards this morning."

Bryan Richards was the head of Houston's FBI office, the biggest in the state.

"What the sheriff shared was right up Cassidy's alley. So we hopped into our vans early this morning, pulled in just a few minutes ago, and here we are. She asked that none of the sheriff's department be in the way. That's when one of the department's detectives said you might already be headed out this way. He said he would try to call you. Cassidy wasn't surprised to find the hornets' nest had been stirred when we got here. She claims you're the least retired detective and biggest busybody she's ever come across. Well, hell, we have to go and keep combing these woods. You all are free to go. In fact, please go, she said."

"What's going to happen to the women, the victims?" Fergie asked.

The guy shrugged, apparently his go-to move. "I think they used to be deported. Many were in their teens when they were lured into this life one way or another. But I think there are support programs to transition them into a more normal life now—you know, medical and mental health help. Some have grown a preference for prostitution, and some become suicidal. Our end is mostly with finding and stopping the trafficking."

"It's just as well, then"—Fergie put her arm around Patty Belle's shoulder—"that this one wasn't part of the turning tricks and such. She just got swept up in the whole mess."

"Oh, I forgot to mention. My name's Harmon Mandleson. I'm second in command, so I'd better get a hustle on. There's a god-awful mess to sort out back there, and it'll be easier if you're long gone. You two should go seek medical attention, pronto. And as for the little girlie there, I didn't even see her."

He and the other men in camo continued their sweep of the woods as they headed toward the motel, where the shooting had stopped. But a lot of shouting was still going on.

"Several of the young women back there got hit in all the shooting. I'm glad we went in and got Patty Belle out, all the same." Fergie looked the girl over. "And for all that, she's pretty unscathed by all that gunfire and is just as perky and glad to be alive as anyone could imagine."

Al chuckled to himself as they picked up the pace on their way back to his truck.

"What's so blasted funny about all this to you? You ought to see yourself. I've seen a freshly slaughtered side of beef that looked less bloody."

"I was just thinking," he said, "that Cav is going to be furious he missed out on this raid and that Cassidy is getting the feather."

"He's probably just as upset about the Kemper Giles part of all this being handled by the sheriff's department as well," she said. "When we get home and are all bandaged up like good little mummies, we can sit over a cup of coffee or a cold beer and discuss how this was all tied together closely enough to come apart at the same time."

Patty Belle looked up at Fergie and smiled. She reached out a hand, and Fergie took it as they made their way through the woods toward Al's truck.

Chapter Twenty-Six

A l answered the doorbell to find Victor Kahlon standing there, holding a large box that smelled awfully good, with the logo for Cooper's BBQ on the side.

"There's some wild-haired rumor going around that you are going to get married today," Victor said. "So the department pitched in with a few things for your reception, which we figured you'd have at home, being the homebody you are. Give me a hand. There are three more boxes in my car and a case of reasonably cheap-ass champagne to carry in."

Tanner had rushed to the door to push his nose at the box, his tail wagging like a crazy metronome. A white wrap sheathed his body, helping his cracked ribs heal.

Al was covered by a fair amount of tape and bandages as well.

Fergie got up from the couch slowly, favoring a leg also wrapped in white. "We certainly are in peak condition for a white wedding."

Maury came clambering up the stairs. "I'll give a hand bringing those boxes in. Bonnie and I barely got beat up at all this time."

As they carried the boxes in, Victor asked Al, "Still going through with the wedding?"

"Yeah. We thought we'd better leap at the chance before we're sucked into some other mess that damn near kills us. I haven't heard much from Clayton, which is actually kind of a blessing. Does he still have his hindquarters up over his back?"

"You of all people know how he is, Al. You may have been right about Rawley, but Clayton is still pissed about how you got there—mostly because he can't wrap his head around your ignoring the proper procedure and the other steps you took to get there."

189

Al waited for Bonnie to come hold the front door open. She was wiping her hands with a towel after puttering around at the kitchen sink.

He looked back at Victor. "I was stressed and pressed for time. I had to use every bit of my thirty years as a detective and the experience and intuition that went with that."

"By the way," Bonnie asked, "have they caught that Rawley fellow yet?"

"Not yet," Victor said. "But you should see all the stuff we got from his place once we had grounds to give it a thorough search. We have enough to put him away for years once we lay hands on him. We also found enough to maybe shut the office doors of half a dozen lower-level ambulance-chasing lawyers."

When the boxes were stacked on a countertop in the kitchen, Bonnie asked, "Can I get you a cup of coffee and maybe a slice of pie?"

"I'd welcome both." Victor eased into a chair at the dining table. "There's a chance I might even be up for a promotion unless I'm considered too much like Al. I hated to even bring it up when all you got out of all this was a fairly frisky roughing up."

"The 'something blue' at the wedding is going to be all the bruises these three have." Bonnie waved a hand toward Al, Fergie, and Tanner.

Patty Belle came up the stairs, carrying the baby. She was grinning like a raccoon that had just found a clam.

Bonnie signed to her and told Victor, "I appreciate you finding us a good attorney to handle Patty Belle becoming a citizen, after which she plans to stay at the house and be part of the family."

Victor's head panned to Al, and he raised an eyebrow.

Al shrugged. "My plans to live out my retirement alone have sure gone to hell on a roller skate."

"We've read and heard reports in the media." Fergie eased into a chair as well, using the table as a support while favoring her leg. "The

The man's right hand pointed at Al, and it held a gun. The hand shook slightly. Al could clearly see a big signet ring, a raised cameo with heavy gold mounting on the man's right forefinger.

Bishop Rawley, somewhat the worse for wear, looked like he'd been sleeping outdoors in his clothes, perhaps in a culvert somewhere. He certainly didn't look happy, nor did he look like he'd come to talk.

He took slow, shaky steps toward Al, his eyes hysterically wide and as fierce as a rabid dog's.

Fergie crumpled to the ground.

Rawley stopped as the barrel moved downward to aim at her where she lay still, then it rose to point at Al once again. His fingers went white around the pistol's grip.

Bam!

But the shot hadn't come from Rawley's gun. His eyes got even wider. He looked down at his chest, dropped his gun with a clatter on the floor, then crumpled atop it.

Al looked down at the .38 Smith & Wesson Chief's Special held in Fergie's extended arm. On her exposed lower leg, he could see the ankle holster.

"You were packing?" Al asked.

"Actually, this is Bonnie's peashooter. It's the 'something borrowed.' She had to get a new one when she never got hers back from those damned Aryans," Fergie said. "Now, give me a hand getting up, would you please? You know how I never want to look remotely my age."

CLAYTON ARRIVED SO quickly that Al wanted to ask if he'd been staked out somewhere near the church, watching and waiting.

"You were getting married? You? Al Quinn?" Clayton came to stand in front of where Al and Fergie were sitting on a front pew. He shook his large head. "Imagine getting married at your seasoned and curmudgeonly stage of life. Why wasn't I invited?"

"I thought we were at odds."

"Hell, I figured, smart as you are, you knew I had a leak in the department I was hoping to plug."

"Who was it?"

"Maddie Sarrison, a department dispatcher we've had for thirteen years. She was keeping Giles informed. She not only knew about his operation but made more money from it than she made at the department. I not only fired her but filed criminal charges, and she's in the department's jail, hoping real hard that the other inmates don't find out she was a cop."

Al leaned out around Clayton to watch the crime scene crew wrestle Rawley into a body bag.

"The pistol he was carrying is an older 7.65 Browning automatic. I suspect, when we check, we'll find it's the same gun Rawley's father had used to commit suicide many years ago. That happened shortly after the son had washed out as a prospective deputy sheriff, yet another reason Rawley might've harbored an animus toward you."

Victor came over to stand beside Clayton. "What are you thinking, boss?"

"I'm thinking we should move this shindig over to Al's house and have the wedding there." His eyes swept the huddled crowd, taking in Patty Belle and the baby. "That way, his dog can be included, too, in this whole wackadoodle family of his."

"That sounds like a good idea to me." Al helped Fergie to her feet. "The best one we've had so far."

With Clayton there, everything felt more right, like having a father present to give away the bride.

"There's plenty to eat," Al said. "No cake, but if I know Bonnie, there's pie."

"There's pie," Bonnie admitted.

"Then let's go," Al said. "It's a fine day for a wedding, and we'll have it by the lake after all." He felt a surge of joy all the way to his toes. "A fine day indeed."

About the Author

Russ Hall is author of fifteen published fiction books, most in hardback and subsequently published in mass market paperback by Harlequin's Worldwide Mystery imprint and Leisure Books. He has also co-authored numerous non-fiction books, most recently *Do You Matter: How Great Design Will Make People Love Your Company* (Financial Times Press, 2009) with Richard Brunner, former head of design at Apple, *Now You're Thinking* (Financial Times Press, 2011), and *Identity* (Financial Times Press, 2012) with Stedman Graham, Oprah's companion.

His graduate degree is in creative writing. He has been a nonfiction editor for major publishing companies, ranging from HarperCollins (then Harper & Row), Simon & Schuster, to Pearson. He has lived in Columbus, OH, New Haven, CT, Boca Raton, FL, Chapel Hill, NC, and New York City. Moving to the Austin area from New York City in 1983.

He is a long-time member of the Mystery Writers of America, Western Writers of America, and Sisters in Crime. He is a frequent judge for writing organizations.

In 2011, he was awarded the Sage Award, by The Barbara Burnett Smith Mentoring Authors Foundation—a Texas award for the mentoring author who demonstrates an outstanding spirit of service in mentoring, sharing and leading others in the mystery writing community. In 1996, he won the Nancy Pickard Mystery Fiction Award for short fiction.

Read more at www.russhall.com.

Unlocking New Worlds

About the Publisher

Dear Reader,

We hope you enjoyed this book. Please consider leaving a review on your favorite book site.

Visit https://RedAdeptPublishing.com to see our entire catalogue.

Don't forget to subscribe to our monthly newsletter to be notified of future releases and special sales.

Made in the USA
Coppell, TX
01 August 2021

59800048R00115